UPSTREAM AT THE MILL

UPSTREAM
AT THE MILL

DENYS VAL BAKER

WILLIAM KIMBER · LONDON

First published in 1981 by
WILLIAM KIMBER & CO. LIMITED
Godolphin House, 22a Queen Anne's Gate,
London, SW1H 9AE

© Denys Val Baker, 1981
ISBN 0 -7183-0098-X

Photoset by
Specialised Offset Services Limited, Liverpool
and printed and bound in Great Britain by
Redwood Burn Limited, Trowbridge & Esher

Contents

I

Autumn at the Mill

Although there can be little doubt that the weather in Cornwall has deteriorated drastically since I first came to live here more than thirty years ago, it would seem that autumns have remained the most constant. Whereas summers now often seem submerged by endless rainy days and winters have become increasingly severe – snows in Cornwall, unheard of three decades ago – autumn somehow still manages to retain the poetic quality of being that 'season of mists and mellow fruitfulness', etc. Perhaps this is one of the reasons why it continues to be a time of great physical and indeed creative activity 'down in the valley' at our old mill house at Tresidder Bottoms.

Another reason, no doubt, is that many of us have but recently returned from a welcome summer break navigating our old boat *Sanu* on its journey homewards towards Cornwall from the Mediterranean. Sun-tanned and full of new vitality, it is only natural that we should be ready and eager for new projects – which at the Mill House seldom seem in short supply. Among these is the perpetual and continuing saga of the resurrection of our water wheel and also, as I described in my last volume, *As the Stream Flows By*, the short sharp shock of spending nearly a hundred man hours erecting Jess's new and Heath Robinsonish greenhouse – not forgetting the traumatic tale of our daughter Demelza's thirty-foot caravan negotiating our narrow potholed lane and ending up beside the bubbling waters of the River Penberth.

Now, in the latest autumn I am contemplating, we found ourselves confronted by a new project altogether: the erection of a studio by our painter son-in-law Alan. For many years now Alan, an art teacher in the London area, had been coming down whenever possible to enjoy the delights of rural Cornish life with us and while here he would often drive off to somewhere like St Ives or Newlyn or Lamorna or Land's End to produce sketches and notes for landscape paintings. At his home in Fulham he had a proper studio where he could work away, but unfortunately at the Mill House we lacked a suitable room. Why not, then, *create* one?

Alan was immediately intrigued by such an idea and it wasn't long before he came up with the ideal and very practical solution – namely to buy one of those large portable wooden buildings regularly advertised in *Exchange and Mart* and have it brought down and set up somewhere in our rambling grounds. Such a building, perhaps featuring some plastic sheets in the roof to provide plenty of natural light, would make an ideal painter's workshop-cum-studio. Some day, too, who knew, it might be useful as a place where he could train budding painters, or perhaps run a summer painting school.

The possibilities were exciting: the practicalities, as ever, formidable. First there was the question of siting. Our land, though consisting largely of trees and rambling rockery, still offered one or two alternatives: a spot high up near the pool that fed our water leat, a vague rather morassy area among the trees lining the river opposite the house, and a curious little peninsula of land forming a bend in the lane which ran past us up to the Tresidder farm of Lady Bolitho. We had always thought of this as an ideal place for a caravan or some such temporary edifice but our experiences with Demelza's travelling monster had made it very clear to us that there were limits to what could be achieved, and we soon realised that this corner site was too high and difficult for a caravan. For a portable building, however, which would arrive in sections and be assembled on the spot, there would appear to be fewer problems.

Or so it seemed. Having made his enthusiastic choice of the site Alan now arranged to come down for a fortnight and work on the necessary clearing and preparation. Never one for doing things the easy way, Alan embarked on an almost maniacal period of enormous physical activity. Day after day he would drive into Penzance and bring back fresh loads of concrete blocks, timbers, cement, sand and unload them all at the foot of the steps leading up to his 'plot'. The latter, of course, required a good deal of equally prodigious work done to it before Alan could even begin laying his foundations. The land was on a slope, which meant first Alan had to dig away about half the area until it was all level. As this involved clearing the roots of several dead and withered trees plus one or two formidable living ones, his task soon assumed herculean proportions. Since the only person around really able to help him, our son Stephen, was very much occupied at the time, Alan did in fact pretty well accomplish his foundation-laying entirely on his own.

For several days he disappeared soon after dawn and we would not see him until after dark; sometimes as his pale worn figure appeared at the kitchen doorway, Jess and I would feel quite worried about his general health and well-being. However there is always a great satisfaction about actual 'doing your own thing' and I fancy Alan really enjoyed that fortnight. At the end not only was the site levelled and cleared, but covered neatly by solid rows of granite blocks and all the requisite beams and frames of wood necessary to form the base of the building. It was a tired but happy Alan who drove back to London to complete the business of acquiring the building and arranging for its despatch to Cornwall.

All this took time, of course – and not a little trouble since the yard from which Alan bought the building appeared perpetually vague about delivery. In the end, growing desperate, Alan remembered our friend Mike Richards, now running his own haulage business at Lelant. Mike frequently made deliveries of Cornish vegetables to Covent Garden and was glad enough to pick up a portable building for a return load. Since the building in all measured some 20 feet by 30 feet this proved to be quite an undertaking even for Mike's giant lorry, but one fine day arrived when his driver came knocking on our door to inform us that 'the building' was indeed standing on his lorry at the end of our lane.

He also informed us that having taken a close look at the size of our lane he realised it would be quite impossible to get the lorry any nearer: all he could do would be to offload the sections and leave them leaning against the hedge at the end of the lane. Fortunately Alan was down for the weekend to supervise operations; equally fortunately Stephen had a handy little Morris Traveller with a roof rack; and that in the end was how Alan and Stephen transferred the portable studio from one end of the lane to the other, by tying each section to the roof rack of the Morris and carrying them along, bumping against the low lying tree branches.

When it came to setting up the portable building we were in for quite a few surprises. Before Alan had begun clearing the corner of land it had seemed a large area; once it was cleared and standing virginally bare it seemed absolutely enormous. And yet, once his foundations were laid and more especially the actual building was erected, we could hardly believe our eyes. The original section of land had completely disappeared beneath the spread of the 30-foot by 20-foot building. Such a tight fit was it all, in fact, that in one corner Alan had to make a small inlet into his building so that it could be laid out over the immovable huge root of an old elm tree, right on a corner of the lawn.

Paradoxically, despite its size the building occupied such a secluded position that viewed from most directions it was hardly discernible. This was partly because on two sides it was cloaked by huge bushes of bamboos which lie clumped around our gardens, and partly because in almost all directions we are overlooked by tall willowy elm and sycamore trees (graceful for most of the year but rather frightening at times of gales, as I shall relate in another chapter). Of course, the building was a low one and its wide sloping roof, covered with weathered roofing felt, soon blended into the background. We had painted Demelza's caravan emerald green so that it was hardly noticeable among the trees. I suggested to Alan the same approach, as we are very fond of our generally uninterrupted vista of green lawns and tall trees, against which the 400-year-old granite walls of the house itself seem to grow out of the ground as naturally as the trees. In the end he plumped for a black creosote style of covering and surprisingly enough this did seem to merge.

Once it was erected, we were all eagerly invited on a tour of inspection of Alan's new baby. I must say everyone was duly taken aback when, opening the small red door at one end, we found ourselves in what could well have been some village hall or similar edifice. Twenty feet by thirty feet is of course quite a size, but I have been into sitting rooms of such a size before now without noticing anything untoward – because, of course, they have been partially filled with furnishings. By contrast Alan's studio stood there stark and bare and therefore seeming huge.

'Well,' I said, looking around in some wonder. 'What's the next step?'

The next sensible step Alan decided, would be to hire some sanding equipment and give the dirty old floorboards a thorough going over. Here he showed more imagination than I would have done, for in fact, almost unbelievably, what had been a very ordinary and rather dreary floor covering changed overnight into a gleaming and glistening vista of polished pinewood, upon which the next day Alan put several coatings of sealant. By the time he had finished the floor would not have disgraced a ballroom, let alone a studio.

With him on his latest journey down, Alan had brought a number of his old paintings and as much equipment as possible, and all these were now spread around, while we contributed a long flat working table and one or two chairs, plus an old divan which at least would make a useful receptacle for models in the future. Very slowly the place began to take on the appearance of a working studio, especially after we had managed to run a cable across for lighting, and installed a couple of paraffin heaters for warmth. Indeed it was seeing the studio lit up like this one night, all cosy and glowing and cheerful, that I think prompted Alan's final impulse before, sadly, he had to return to work in London.

'I know – let's have a party to christen the new studio.'

There were in fact several reasons prompting Alan's decision other than his own wish to celebrate, and one of the most important of these had to do with the return to our midst of an old friend who had spent nearly three years sailing half way round the world, but finally reached home harbour.

This was Llewellyn Baker, son of our old friend Frank and Kate Baker, and oft-time companion on our *Sanu* trips, on one of which, around the Dodecanese Isles, he was in charge of our highly idiosyncratic Kelvin diesel engine (at one stage taking the whole thing to pieces and putting it together again faultlessly). The last time we had seen Llewellyn was during our cruise along the beautiful shores of Southern Turkey. Llewellyn had joined us at Marmaris, bringing with him his very bright little eight-year-old boy, Ikey. They were on a one-way trip out to India where Llewellyn's ex-wife Bobby, now remarried, lived at Ponticherry with Llew's other child, his daughter Nell.

Ever since the unfortunate break-up of their marriage Llewellyn seemed to have spent most of his life travelling between England and India in order to maintain contact with his children. Being rather vague about money he invariably seemed to end up hitching most of the way, and this was to be no exception. At a spot just beyond Fethiye and not far from Antalya, Alan rowed Llew and Ikey ashore, both heavily clad with rucksacks and sleeping bags, and there, rather worriedly, we left them – off on the high road through Turkey and Iran towards distant India.

We did well to be worried. Just before leaving I had given Llewellyn a little money to help on his way. Within a day he managed to get robbed of this small amount and he and Ikey were left near to destitution. Yet somehow they managed. It is my own theory that Llewellyn secretly feels happier in such desperate situations. Certainly it does seem that whenever he is stranded in this way people respond most kindly and a real common humanity emerges, as in this instance when villagers took them in and gave them food and helped them on their way.

To cut that long story rather short, Llewellyn and Ikey

reached Ponticherry, where rather to his disgust Ikey was sent to school with his sister, while his father settled for a while in a reclusive hut in some woods outside for a period of fasting and meditation. It was about this time that the object which was so dramatically to affect Llewellyn's life for the next three years made its fleeting appearance off the shores of Ponticherry.

This was the peace boat *Fri*, an old fashioned Baltic trading schooner belonging to a young American, David, who had formed around him a loose-knit idealistic crew of peace-lovers – rather on the lines of the Greenpeace boats – and was now making a return voyage from New Zealand, where they had been protesting against the French atomic explosions. The boat in fact was only anchored briefly at Ponticherry, but it so happened that Llewellyn was down at the beach at the time it arrived and could not resist swimming out to take a look.

Once aboard and having met the crew and gathered the idea of what it was all about, he said eagerly, 'Have you room for myself and my young son?'

'Yes, of course,' said David.

I don't suppose he ever had reason to regret his prompt acceptance, for in fact not only has Llewellyn got his mate's ticket (earned via the hard school of Newlyn fishing port) but his whole personality and body might have been designed for the sea. When I heard later of Llew's settling aboard this old sailing schooner I could not help a momentary pang of regret, for knowing his romantic nature I guessed that henceforth sailing would always hold the greatest part in his affections, and that never again would he feel quite the same about our dieselly old tub.

However I could hardly begrudge him the marvellous experience that followed. He and Ikey quickly boarded the boat with their few belongings and setting sail at once for Sri Lanka, where they spent several weeks working on the boat, including a most complicated 'careening' process by which the boat was tied by its mast to the shore and pulled over almost horizontally to enable the bottom to be cleaned and anti-fouled. After many ups and downs the *Fri* finally sailed off across the Indian Ocean for Mozambique where more weeks were spent and where, incidentally, they were treated most hospitably by this much maligned Marxist state – in contrast to their treatment later in Mauritius and in South Africa, where they were not even allowed to land! Perhaps the South African unfriendliness had some justification since the *Fri was* bound for Nambibia, where they planned to distribute leaflets protesting against the way the peoples of that small country had been treated by their South African 'neighbours'. In the end, through a complicated series of circumstances, *Fri* was never able to make much impact at Nambibia, and was forced to sail on to Angola, and then later across to the Azores ...

Altogether they had been travelling halfway round the world for nearly three years before one momentous day Frank and Kate, watching out at the Lizard Point, spied the tall masts on the horizon and rushed off to Falmouth to organise a champagne welcoming party for their much beloved second son.

All this I have recounted at some length to explain why, besides wishing to christen his new building, Alan was also greatly pleased to be welcoming home an old shipmate – and in fact it was decided that the party should combine an invitation to the entire crew of the *Fri*. It was a gesture which was particularly welcomed at the time, because unfortunately ever since arriving in Falmouth *Fri* had not exactly been made welcome by the local authorities. These officials are only human I suppose and viewed with considerable disfavour the presence in the centre of the port of a badly leaking old sailing schooner with what could only be called a very motley crew, including what would be regarded as hippies and beatnik types. David, the captain and owner of the boat, was obviously a very experienced sailor and able to deal with any harbour-master, but it had been made clear that *Fri*'s stay at Falmouth had to be a very temporary one and David was already desperately looking for some permanent winter berth where they could work on the boat (later, by good fortune, they found just such a berth up the Helford Estuary near Gweek).

When the day of the party came Alan and Gill and the rest of the family spent an hour or two tarting up the new studio, putting in gay curtains and laying out chairs and cushions, while someone else brought back a carload of beer and wine from Penzance. Since Jess and I firmly regarded this as Alan's party and no worry of our own we settled down initially in our kitchen.

At about six o'clock, two or three hours before the party started, we were a little disconcerted to find a rather bedraggled set of people filing up the drive and banging on our kitchen door. This, it transpired, was the crew of *Fri*, headed by their dark-bearded, softly spoken captain, David. We did not at first realise that they were in fact rather hungry, since they had been having a pretty frugal time. We were really in no position to feed about a dozen extra people, but eventually we managed to sort this out by some of the crew going up to Stephen's chalet, some to Alan's, and David and one or two others settling at our round table in the kitchen, where we managed to give them omelettes and a glass of wine while we listened to their truly vivid sailors' tales.

Whatever else one might feel about them they were basically a group of ordinary young people who had gone out and sailed the high seas in the face, very often, of great dangers, and as the evening wore on we warmed to them – especially to David, who had great charm and perception. I could see that our daughter Genevieve also warmed to David quite considerably, but alas – as with so many of the 'white knights' that loom on Genevieve's romantic horizon – this one was only fleetingly around, and soon would be wending his way back to America, and other worlds.

Nevertheless, for that evening at least, we all trooped over to Alan's new studio, and there enjoyed a lively boisterous party, during which more than once I found myself anxiously eyeing the floor which seemed to be going up and down like a yo-yo under the strain of nearly thirty pairs of feet. Still it survived, and the drink survived, and the music roared on, and one way and another the party was a great success ... going on all night and ending up with leisurely cups of coffee at breakfast time around our Aga, before, a little sadly, I think, the crew of the *Fri* departed back to their leaking boat.

Llewellyn stayed on after the others, and I had the chance to ask him what he planned for the future. Alas, poor Llew – he is like a creature in a perpetual storm, blown hither and thither. Even at that moment he was becoming involved in an emotional entanglement which was to cause all kinds of problems, and I could well sympathise when, on a later date, he declared morosely that he thought the best thing he could do was get back to sea. This in fact is how I see his life: if ever there was a born seaman and traveller it is Llewellyn – so wherever he may be, good luck to him.

Our visitors from *Fri* made quite a powerful impact upon various members of our family. For several weeks afterwards it seemed there were always car-loads zooming off to Falmouth for a reunion or some party or a jazz session, Melza with her bongos, Genny with her sax, Stephen with his guitar. They were a happy-go-lucky lot on *Fri*, idealistic too, and we hoped that things would work out well for them – as indeed they seemed to be doing when we heard that a French film crew had come over with the idea of making a full-length film about *Fri*'s exploits, when they entered the forbidden zone around the French atomic tests out in the Pacific. In these terrifying days there can be no doubt that every protest helps, lest we all get blown to kingdom come by our trigger-happy politicians. That is why I shall always feel that individual protests, such as are made by *Fri* or more notably still perhaps by *Rainbow Warrior*, with its dinghy loads of protesters stationing themselves between whales and their hunters – these sort of personal physical examples are well worth a hundred mouthed protests. To do what these protesters do requires the sort of courage that everyone can appreciate.

Back once again to our everyday life, we settled into a long period of practical activities about the Mill House. Something which had always been in our mind from the first day we arrived and saw the clusters of trees enclosed in our property was the desirability of one day possessing a chain-saw of our own. On one or two occasions we had hired a saw from a local firm but for some reason these ventures had not been entirely successful; too often the machine broke down, thus wasting valuable money and time. Obviously it would be far better to have our own machine with whose workings we could become technically familiar.

This is what we now decided upon. In fact the whole family not only made the decision, but sportingly came in on the financial side, each making a contribution – a sensible enough way of going about things, since it seemed likely that most were going to spend longer and longer enjoying the delights of country life at Tresidder. Certainly one of the greatest of those delights is the sight of a lovely log fire roaring away to keep out the chill of winter days – though in fact another reason we wanted a chain saw of our own was to help Stephen in his eternal long term plan for rebuilding the wheel (there were several dead trees around which with a chain saw he could soon have down and cut up to size for making wheel paddles).

After studying various advertisements we decided against an electric saw and in favour of the sort that have their own small two stroke petrol engines – further, we resolutely avoided thoughts of saving money by getting a small saw and plumped instead for a 20-inch one which would enable us to tackle best the biggest of our trees. After ringing round the various dealers we found one over at Helston that had a wide range of toughly made Homelite saws, and one fine day Stephen and Jess went over there and managed by great good luck to pick up a bargain, a 20-inch saw that was slightly shop soiled and greatly reduced.

As both Jess and I remained somewhat nervous of chain saws we were relieved to find that Stephen, who would be the principal user, shared our concern and that he was even prepared to go to the lengths of attending a special evening class put on by the makers of the chain-saw where they showed films and slides and answered questions about safe handling, etc. With a lethal weapon like a chain-saw, better be prepared than sorry.

When the chain-saw arrived it proved to be quite a handsome instrument, painted a bright red and full of latent power. Stephen tried it out on a few fallen logs and it appeared to slice through these like a knife through butter. Greatly encouraged we began our onslaught on the first of several of our elm trees which had been stricken with the dreaded plague. In this instance the tree was one of three standing by our front gate, only a short distance from the bungalow of our only neighbour, Sheila Ley.

Not wanting to make a bad first impression by accidentally dropping a tree upon her bedroom roof we called in the aid of a friend, Nathan Kemp, a painter living up the road. He had once worked for the Forestry Commission and knew all about felling trees. What's more he amply proved this by bringing along a very long and stout rope, tying the tree top to a corner of the house and then supervising Stephen while he cut steadily into the base of the tree.

Jess and I stood holding our breath as the top of the tree began to sway, fearful that it might go the wrong way and take the rope with it ... fortunately all was well and at the appropriate moment, with that terrible dying sound of all falling trees, the tree came crashing down not on Sheila's house but right across our front drive. Moments later Stephen was straddling it, the light of battle in his eyes, cutting up the huge trunk into more sizeable portions. After that the plan was to put a portion at a time into the back of his old Morris and take them off to a sawmill to be cut up into short lengths to make paddles.

Such a plan, alas, was not well suited to Stephen's erratic temperament as he would take a couple of trunks and then leave things for a week or two, with the result that – as ever – our famous wheel seemed destined to remain something of a dream.

We were by no means short of other ideas, however, where the chain-saw was concerned. Initially, one assumed it would be useful in producing firewood: being the person mainly responsible for laboriously sawing up endless rows of logs, I was a little dismayed to find that while the chain-saw could cut down trees to a certain size, it was not practical to use it for cutting up very small logs, and that I still had to do these

by hand! Still, as everyone was always telling me, the exercise
was good for me, and indeed so it was, and I found it quite
satisfying each day to fill up the spaces beside our lovely old
fire, with neatly cut new logs. And of course the wood *was*
lovely for burning, being usually dead wood that had lain
around for some time – not so much the elm, but the sycamore
in particular.

Apart from logs, we now entered upon our era of great
creative activity in a new field. It was Jess's idea originally, I
think. She suggested to Stephen, as he tackled one particularly
large fallen tree, why not slice it up into thin slices with the
idea that we might make cheeseboards out of the pieces?
Intrigued, Stephen quickly sliced off twenty lengths. Jess bore
these off in triumph to the kitchen, laid them out on a table,
and began sanding and trimming them, as well as peeling the
outer bark off the rims. Since the general shape of the trunk
was not a symmetrical circle, but more of a wiggly oval, the
result was ideal for a cheeseboard: indeed, so quickly did the
Tresidder craftsmen and women work, that by the end of the
day we had nearly a dozen cheeseboards shaped and trimmed
and sanded and ready for the sealing with Bourneseal, which
we still had to buy.

Making the cheeseboards was not entirely a casual idea.
The fact was that recently Demelza and Genevieve had hired a
stall at the Portobello Market in London, and it seemed quite
reasonable to suppose that there they would be able to sell
hand-carved cheeseboards from crafty Cornwall. On their
next visit they approved very much of the idea, and Genevieve
even introduced a variation by using a soldering iron to burn
decorative patterns upon one or two of the cheeseboards. The
fact that in the long run these decorated cheeseboards were
the *only* ones ever to sell is, I fear, some sort of commentary
upon our lack of business acumen, and perhaps also a tribute
to Genevieve's natural talents for decoration.

Creativity must have been very much in the air at this time.
With the aid of a slightly reluctant Gina, Jess had embarked
upon yet another scheme for a craft line which might sell in
Portobello Road. When in Spain the previous summer she had

bought a lampshade that had intrigued her, a complete oval shape made of nothing but string, and yet standing up straight and firm. She had discovered the method by which it was produced, and now proceeded to set up her own little mini-factory at Tresidder.

Briefly the work consisted of buying endless rolls of strong string, several packets of balloons, and large tins of paste. You first blew up a balloon, threading the cord through a hole in the paste tin so that by pulling the string through it got really sticky, and then started winding it round the outside of the balloon, crossing and criss-crossing in all kinds of patterns until the whole balloon surface was completely covered. The whole contraption was then hung up to dry for several days, the theory being that at the end of that period, when the glue had completely dried so that the cord was still and hard, you just punctured the balloon – and hey presto, you had a magical string lampshade!

At least that was the idea! Soon our kitchen was festooned with global objects all over the place, some in varying degrees of size as unfortunately not every balloon remained fully expanded! Personally I inclined to a sneaking idea that neither the cheeseboards nor the lampshades were somehow likely to be great money spinners ... and in this instance I was only too right. All the same we had some amusing evenings sitting in our kitchen as the nights began drawing in, working away at our new craft! What a pity that it never really, as the saying goes, got off the ground. Does any reader, I wonder, require a few dozen interesting shapes in hardened string?

II

A Writer's Life

Cutting down trees, slicing up cheeseboards, making balloon lampshades and constantly thinking about possibilities of reviving the water wheel were by no means the limit of our activities at the Mill House that autumn. Jess had come back from her away-from-it-all wander round the Balearic Isles full of renewed vigour and determination to extend her gardening schemes. The previous winter had witnessed the considerable achievement of setting up her own new greenhouse and (although catastrophe lay waiting for this and many other efforts) for the moment she was able to indulge herself in planting new seed beds, clearing out old ones, and constantly thinking up new ideas like persuading Stephen to extend the water line leading to his chalet further up the hillside to provide a decent water supply for 'the plot', as Jess's own vegetable garden high above our house was usually known.

Thus supplied with a very necessary raw material Jess cast her mind around, literally for fresh fields to conquer. It must have been about this time that she made the momentous decision to acquire yet another new implement: after the chain-saw – the rotavator. Here again past experiences of hiring this highly desirable horticultural aid had not been happy, and for exactly the same reason as with the hired chain-saw: somehow other people's possessions never seem to work as well in a stranger's hands (a truism we discovered later on when, much against our wishes, we were prevailed on by a friend to hire him our own chain-saw to deal with an emergency tree fall: two days later he came back with a long face and quite a complaining attitude – with the entire chain-saw blunt and ruined). Some years ago while living at the Old

Sawmills we had picked up a second-hand rotavator and used it with somewhat mixed success. This time Jess was determined we would start life with a new rotavator, untouched by infidel hands.

Once again there began a search through the advertisements, in gardening magazines and the local papers, and once again we were lucky in that Jess managed to discover a local agent for the make she fancied, the Merry Tiller, so that she was able to go over and view the machine in action. At first she came back marvelling at the performance of man not machine. Apparently the man handling the rotavator was seventy-five years old and as fit as a fiddle, embarking on all sorts of formidable physical feats – what a pity she was married to a weak and useless creature of sixty-two, etc. After getting this out of her system she managed to convince Stephen and I that the Merry Tiller sounded a good buy, and so we bought it. At least we paid out some money and sat back and waited: as ever in these cases the wait seemed interminable, but finally one day a bright glistening new blue Merry Tiller rotavator stood literally panting outside our front door (after Stephen had excitedly poured in some petrol and oil and given the engine a swing just to make sure everything was in working order).

A Merry Tiller standing outside the Mill House front door was one thing: a Merry Tiller 300 feet up on the side of our sloping field, we soon discovered, was quite another. Certainly Jess found the machine far too heavy to propel along and even Stephen, strong as he is, had all his work cut out to coax the machine up the winding lane and into the field. Even there the ground was still on a slope and we began to despair that we had made some dreadful mistake. To this day Jess herself has considerable difficulty in handling the machine, but fortunately Stephen finally acquired the knack, and I must admit that under his direction the Tiller was soon performing valiant feats, churning up stretches of tangled jungle in no time at all. Soon, to Jess's delight, the area of her vegetable patch had been almost doubled and before she could bear to give poor Stephen a respite she had him levelling out yet another area designed to be her new fruit garden.

Meantime, allowing for my total uselessness in agricultural activities, I had at last been given a project considered to be within my limited means.

'You can build me a garden shed. Just over there, near the greenhouse. It will be an ideal place for keeping the rotavator and tools and so on.'

Building sheds has always been something to which I am reasonably partial, so I set to on my project with great enthusiasm. As with so many projects at the Mill House it was not to be supposed that I should have the advantage of new materials or anything like that. No, my job was to go around the 'estate' scrounging old planks and make do with these as my materials. Surprisingly enough, I managed to do just that. In the process I found myself dismantling a once impressive verandah surrounding the entrance to an old derelict caravan up near the water leat, as well as nicking a plank or two from Stephen's private hoard. At one stage I looked hard and longingly at some planks stored under Demelza's caravan, but decided I could not face the possible wrath of my rather voluble Virgo daughter, so I left them alone.

By the time I had carried all these planks up to the top of the field I found I had more than enough material for the job in hand. I also learned, regrettably, that my ancient frame simply wasn't up to so much of this physical activity. That is to say, ever since my thrombosis two years before I had found climbing hills represented a truly fearsome prospect, and the fact that nobody outside of my own body appeared able to appreciate my problem was of little help. I knew that this constant climbing up the steep pathways carrying planks was not doing me any good, and indeed I was to pay for it by a series of bouts of illness in due course. Nevertheless, I had the grim satisfaction of knowing that the materials for my project were at last assembled, and in due course I was able to apply myself to the actual erection process.

Here again I had to run the gauntlet of an extremely critical employer, since Jess and I have diametrically opposite views on how to tackle almost any job, but I went on doggedly with my task until at last I was able to stand back and survey, not without some pride, a finished garden hut – admittedly no beauty, but a fairly solid and practical hut into which, as I proceeded to demonstrate, there was just room to wheel the Merry Tiller. A line of nails hammered into the side of one wall provided positions for hanging all the tools; finally a shelf at the back for odds and ends – and my task was over, I felt.

'What about a door?' said Jess morosely. 'You haven't put a door on.'

Sadly this was true. It was a problem I never totally overcame, owing to the fact that like so many of my previous constructions, my hut was not on the level, indeed on quite a slope. The best I could do was fix on an old door taken off what had once been the Elsan closet of the old caravan. This hung at an angle of 45 degrees so that a certain area of the hut was still uncovered, but at least it protected most of the Tiller from any blasts of east wind – and anyway our prevailing wind was south-western (a fact we were to discover in some alarm a few months later).

What with all this intermittent gardening activity, broken by a series of bouts of illness, I was finding it difficult to do much writing. Occasionally readers of my books have written in recent years complaining that a note of sadness appears to have crept into my narratives. It would be rather surprising if this were not so. I suppose in everyone's life there is a classic instance of a single misfortune which has sent things off on a tangent. My own instance had certainly been when I had a gall bladder operation which had achieved nothing so far as any improvement in health was concerned but did have the irreversible after-effect of a thrombosis (blood clotting following an operation). If I appear sad about this it does not seem unreasonable. Prior to this unfortunate development I was relatively strong physically, had hardly been near hospital for fifty years, used to go for long country walks of six or seven miles – in short I was a reasonably fit man. Ever since the thrombosis my life had been woefully conditioned: steep hills are virtually impossible, long walks equally out, and my horizons generally curtailed.

Jess and I would have interminable arguments about all

this. Her attitude is conditioned by her own character and temperament. She is a get up and go type, to whom any admission of defeat is anathema: I on the other hand tend towards automatic pessimism and though I freely admit to being some sort of hypochondriac I cannot accept that because of this I do not, and quite frequently, suffer from pain and illness. As I have explained before, I have always been more than willing to make efforts to find cures, in pursuit of which I had seen London quacks, local homoeopathics, all kinds of medico marvels. Soon I shall probably embark on the acupuncture path. In the meantime Genevieve's Tibetan doctor has just sent me a rather alarming looking packet of Tibetan mineral pills for relieving my ailments. Ah, yes, it would be quite funny – if, alas, it wasn't rather sad.

Possibly this pessimistic state of mind on the part of one growing old (gracefully or otherwise) is not helped by one of the hard facts of life – the steady disappearance of so many of one's contemporaries. Just recently this had been brought home to me with quite a shock by the news of the death of another friend of ours, 'Little Jane', Jane Gilbert, whom all of twenty years ago we had known in St Ives. Indeed it had been at one of our parties at St Christopher's that we introduced her to the painter Dick Gilbert, with whom she was to spend much of the rest of her life, and by whom she had two children. It was Dick now who rang us up to tell us the sad news that Jane had suddenly died of a heart attack at the early age of 53, and that the funeral would be held at Penzance Borough Cemetery Chapel.

Like Jess, I am an instinctive believer in the old adage, 'bury your dead' – that is to say, one should always attend friends' funerals if possible both as a mark of respect and as some sort of farewell gesture. This proved to be a rather strange occasion in many ways. Over recent years Jess and I had really rather lost touch with Jane, though now and then we would encounter her diminutive form in Market Jew Street.

Perhaps this had been the experience of several other people at the funeral, for it was a strange conglomeration of ghosts from the past, people we no longer saw much – indeed one might almost have made the macabre joke, 'Hullo, we only meet at funerals now'. There was Sydney Graham and his wife Nessie, once more involved in my life, now ghosts indeed (as I must be to them): and, rather surprisingly, one or two other figures from the past like Tony Shiels and Vernon Rose, both now living over at Falmouth. There was Robert Brennan, a local painter, whom again we hardly ever saw; and one or two more familiar figures like Biddy Picard and Janet Gibbs. Altogether I suppose there must have been about thirty of us crowded into the tiny chapel for a brief and rather soulless service, before forming a winding procession to the graveside.

It was a sad and forlorn occasion. Nothing really personal was said in the chapel; the incumbent had obviously never known Jane and the whole thing seemed appallingly anonymous and helped to solidify in me some ideas I had long had floating at the back of my mind. Briefly, if at all humanly possible when my own time comes I would like to avoid all that anonymity – for me, though I won't be there to appreciate it, I would prefer an ending more romantically in tune with the elements. Somewhere in the recesses of my mind I had it all literally worked out: a cremation with a personal few words by an old friend, a journey to Newlyn, and finally a trip out in a fishing boat to somewhere in Mount's Bay where my ashes could be scattered to the wild sea's bosom.

In my own mind I had even quite clearly in mind the fisherman I would like to perform this little task – and thereby, in more senses than one, lies a story. Although I had long harboured this general idea for celebrating my own ending, and although the fisherman in question is someone I know quite well and see quite frequently, I have somehow never been able to get round to broaching what is after all rather a delicate matter. Suddenly, after Jane's funeral, when I went home and sat down and thought about it all, I became totally diverted by seeing that here, surely, I had the makings of a good short story. I had indeed, and what's more I sat down there and then and wrote the whole thing off in a couple of hours. I called it 'Funeral Arrangements', and told the story rather as above, through the eyes of the prospective deceased, describing the husband and wife being too embarrassed ever to bring up the subject to the fisherman. In my story I gave a twist by having the husband read a headline in the paper one morning that the fisherman had been drowned at sea, an ironic ending indeed. I am glad to say that no such fate has befallen my friend – but I still haven't quite managed to bring up the matter yet!

Apart from an occasional very short piece like 'Funeral Arrangements' I find that I seldom write short stories these days. One reason for this of course, is that I have written so many in the past; indeed the number runs into more than 300, practically all published in one magazine or another. Now from time to time I very much enjoy sorting them out and bringing out an occasional collection. It is a curious, perhaps Pavlovian, reaction to this activity that invariably I seem to feel prompted to write one or two new stories at such times – however, as I say, by and large I feel my short story days are over. In some ways this is regrettable since I have always locked on the short story as perhaps the highest form of literary art, and nothing has given me such personal satisfaction as the successful completion of a really satisfying story.

All the same perhaps one can have too much of a good thing, and in recent years I have found more challenge in moving into the field of novel writing – with, of course, articles as the main bread and butter line. Personally I have never expected to make much impact with novels, but one which I wrote two years ago, *Barbican's End*, proved successful enough to merit a reprint – which from a publisher of Peter Kimber's caution I feel is accolade indeed! I have described elsewhere, in *A Family For All Seasons*, how the idea for *Barbican's End* originally came to me, about twenty years ago – the conception of a doomed village on the edge of the wild Cornish coast, a fairly dramatic tale leading to its inevitable climax – and how through all our house moves some instinct made me keep my notes and half written chapters, so that, more recently, I was able to tackle the whole thing and carry it through to the end.

When, after the appearance of *Barbican's End*, Peter Kimber asked me to do another novel I found what seemed a good idea very quickly to hand – namely a book using the magical setting of our old home at the Old Sawmills, Fowey, telling the tale of a girl inheriting such an old place and then finding various characters (for various reasons) trying to interfere with her taking over her inheritance. In my new-found confidence, rather naively perhaps, I envisaged putting a sheet of virginal paper in the typewriter and rattling off this new novel – and indeed I did manage to write the first two or three chapters. Then a strange thing happened: no matter how I went about things, nor from what angle, and despite all attempts at re-writing, changing angles, etc. – I got stuck.

At the time the thought did not immediately occur to me but the other day I was flipping through *An Old Mill by the Stream*, the first of my autobiographies written for Kimber's, in which I described how we came to leave the Old Sawmills and move west to Tresidder – and suddenly the penny clicked. A good deal of that early volume is an attempt to analyse the very strange, almost psychic way in which the Old Sawmills and its atmosphere began to weigh down upon me, turning me into quite a neurotic state to such an extent that I began to feel fearful I would never escape from that beautiful, haunting and yet to me rather deadly place.

Of course! Was it not possible that even ten years later, the moment I foolishly attempted to make some return, even if only in my imagination, the same subterranean forces would come into play? Fanciful perhaps: but if you had ever spent any time at the Old Sawmills, nothing would have seemed too fanciful.

Only the other day I read or heard that Tony Cox, who bought the house from us, recently went to live in another property nearby, using the Old Sawmills solely as a centre for his recording business ... I knew too that earlier occupants seldom stayed there more than a few years, like myself. There *must* be something behind all this sort of behaviour pattern.

Mind you, at the mere mention of that familiar rather haunting name, the Old Sawmills, great waves of nostalgia can come seeping over, like the Atlantic swell at Sennen (and just as dangerous I guess). The feeling was especially enhanced for me one evening when, quite by chance, I switched on a Westward TV arts programme and found myself watching an attractive brunette wandering through what was unmistakably the wild woodland paths of the Old Sawmills, while in the background a pleasing voice sang a top of the pops song about the child of the year. What I was seeing, and hearing, it transpired, was Lesley Duncan, a leading rock vocalist of the seventies who had recently married Tony Cox. The programme was featuring a hit song she had made and the producer had had the very sensible idea of using the beautiful background to accompany the song track. So, while one version of Lesley Duncan sat very serene and immaculate in the studio being interviewed, another wilder and more down to earth Lesley in jeans and jersey, went marching with obvious delight along those paths once so familiar – finally running down the slope by the house to the magical lagoon leading off the Fowey River, into which so often in the past we rowed our old dinghies. Ah yes, at such a moment I envied Tony Cox and Lesley Duncan all that magic – but only, really, for the moment. If there is one thing, sadly, that age and experience does teach it is that in life you simply cannot go back – or at least successfully.

And so to turn forward, or at least return to the present, I might dwell just briefly on that other outlet for what literary talent I have, namely my work on articles, or in other words journalism. For someone with a life now conditioned somewhat by bouts of illness, short articles are the obvious answer. They can be thought up and written usually in a single day, and so are more likely to get done than longer works. Apart from that, I do find article-writing both interesting and stimulating. Not surprisingly, after more than thirty years in Cornwall during which time I ran the *Cornish Review* and have written quite extensively about the county, I quite often get asked by various magazines for articles about some aspect of the county. Not long ago the *Connoisseur* wanted a piece on the original Newlyn School of artists, headed by

Stanhope Forbes and T.C. Gotch, and since I had originally written on this period in an early book *Britain's Art Colony by the Sea*, I was happy to oblige. This was about the same time that the Newlyn Art Gallery had organised a bit retrospective exhibition of the work of the Newlyn painters so that I was able to borrow some excellent photographs taken by Reg Watkiss of some of those early rather marvellous paintings – among them 'The Rain It Raineth Every Day' by Norman Garstin. 'The Drinking Place' by Stanhope Forbes and 'Girl in a Cornish Garden' by T.C. Gotch. The *Connoisseur* did us proud with an eight-page feature, and altogether this was a most satisfying commission.

Many articles, of course, one embarks on without a commission, since, again out of sheer experience, it is not usually difficult to hit the right note for a particular publication. Personally I enjoy as much variety as possible and Cornwall is only one of many subjects I have covered. Others include Italian wines, old motor cars, the work of local rat catchers, the history of trial by jury, islands of the Mediterranean, portraits of Christina Rossetti and Lady Jane Grey, of Virginia Woolf (in Cornwall, that one), the story of a famous chess hoax, a light hearted piece about bank managers, a ditto about doctors, a nostalgic memory of our round table at the Mill House and all the events associated with it – plus, of course, numerous accounts of various cruises in our old boat *Sanu*. That reads like a pretty catholic list, possibly too much so, but then they say variety is the spice of life and one of the attractions about regular article writing is that it keeps the mind active and stimulated. Then again, I always find it an interesting challenge to tackle some entirely new subject. Following this pattern, over recent years I have written a portrait of 'My Flying Father' for the magazine *Aeroplane*, an article about 'the pianos in my life' for a musical publication, and an off-beat profile of Sue Barker, the British tennis star, using her partly as a peg on which to hang my eternal fascination with the one game which still rivets my ageing attention.

Like most forms of authorship journalism is always

something of a gamble which I suppose is one of its attractions to me. Sometimes though one can't help feeling the dice are rather unfairly loaded. Many years ago I used to sell dozens of stories to a radio programme – indeed over the years they broadcast more than a hundred. In recent years, particularly after the editor I dealt with left, I found to my exasperation that not a single story of mine was being accepted, year after year after year. Since someone who has had a hundred stories broadcast is hardly a novice and might reasonably expect some acceptances I endeavoured, politely, to remonstrate, only to receive in reply what might be called official brush-offs. Somewhat stung by this treatment I sorted out a number of stories which had in the past been accepted and broadcast, had them freshly typed and given new titles, and over a period submitted those one by one. Every single one was returned with a printed rejection slip. After that even I gave up! ... though I did not give up in another case of a somewhat similar nature. In this latter instance it was the newspaper *The Guardian*, a bastion of liberalism and our daily newspaper ever since the demise of the late lamented *News Chronicle*. For a person of my outlook and inclinations *The Guardian* would seem a natural outlet, yet over about fifteen years of fairly regular submissions everything came monotonously back, rejected. One day, out of sheer curiosity, I wrote an article under a nom de plume, and sent that off. The same week it appeared in *The Guardian*!

All this is of no special interest except perhaps to explain to the ordinary reader a little of the reason why writers do appear to be, and indeed often become, rather paranoiac. Can you, perhaps, blame us? The same sort of examples could be given in another field altogether, the actual sale and distribution of books. Like the author himself, naturally publishers are only too eager to obtain the widest circulation of the books they produce. Only too often, unfortunately, it really seems as if the main obstacles standing in their way are those they should automatically be entitled to look upon as their allies. I will say nothing here about the librarians, those doughty but happily in the end unsuccessful opponents of the long delayed but finally triumphant (if somewhat bowdlerised) Public Lending Rights Bill. After all, some of my best friends are librarians and our local one is a very pretty lady indeed! About booksellers I could say a lot but had better not! Every author's dream of the ideal bookseller is some fatherly figure whose whole life is devoted to books, and who handles your latest volume with reverence. In real life, sadly, I have found that such creatures are non-existent, and that one's books are much more likely to sell regularly and well in some vast emporium run almost like a supermarket than in the closeted and often cloying atmosphere of some pretentious and rather precious arty bookshop.

But enough of paranoia. Let us return to the more important business of writing itself, and the novel with which eventually I came to follow *Barbican's End*. This again was something I had had at the back of my mind for a long time, a subject which has always drawn me strangely, namely the effect of someone whose mind is not quite normal upon the people around them. I touched on this once in a story, 'All Things Bright and Beautiful', which was included in a collection, *Echoes of the Cornish Cliffs*. Now suddenly, casting around for a replacement for my Old Sawmills novel, I remembered an earlier plot about a brother and sister living partly in a fantasy world – and so I wrote *Karenza*, using as my title one of my favourite Cornish words, which means basically, thy love. (Demelza, the name we gave to our first daughter, has an equally delightful meaning, thy sweetness.) In some sort of way I felt that *Karenza* carried on the general brooding inexplicable theme of *Barbican's End*, and hope the reader will feel the same.

Like quite a few of my short stories, so the idea of *Karenza*, going back quite a long way into the roots of my own past, derived to some extent from outside Cornwall. This has seemed to be the pattern of my writing life for several decades. The fact is that with many creative people the seeds of most of their work are often laid very early on in their life, though they may only come to fruition much later. In this sense for me the most formative years of my life as a writer were undoubtedly the ten years or so I spent either living or visiting my family home up on the coast of North Wales. Up there, in a setting where the sea lapped at long golden sands on the one hand, and vast mountain ranges reared up to the sky on the other, I would have been most unimaginative if I did not respond to such elemental stimulation.

After all, among other things, I am Welsh, anyway; and mother's family went back many generations in the life of Llanfairfechan, near Bangor, while my father's family originally came from Anglesey. Curiously enough once they had left the area neither my father or mother ever seemed interested in returning – this, paradoxically, just about the time when all my romantic urges were taking me summer after summer on the long journey Wales-wards. It was in Wales that I experienced all the pangs of first loves, all the poignancy of broken romances, and I suppose some part of me can never escape from that background. But then, on the other side of the coin, it has seemed perfectly logical that for the past thirty-five years I have removed myself from one Celtic world to another, so in a way I have simply carried on the general pattern of a continuing approach to writing.

What I am trying to say is that as one might put it, the Welsh connection has been no detraction to my later development as a writer in Cornwall – quite the reverse in fact. Many ideas which originally germinated in my mind all those long years ago and then suddenly returned in fuller bloom down here in Cornwall have been easy to put down on paper because, basically, the two worlds are so *similar*. In Cornwall the sea is wilder and more vitally a part of everyday life, but then in Wales the brooding mountains are more majestically a part of that daily existence. Each area is fundamentally impregnated with a haunting sense of the past, of the total mystery of life, and so I have never found any problem about being a Welshman settled in Cornwall, or for that matter someone in Cornwall whose mind often returns to Wales and its images.

This business of atmosphere interests me greatly as a writer, as I feel that whatever qualities I may have in the creative field are for capturing a sense of atmosphere, the feeling of place, rather than particular characters. Now and then I like to feel I have managed to bring to life a person – like Josie Pengelly in *Barbican's End*, or Karenza in the novel of that name, or Nell, the wife in an earlier novel, *A Company of Three*. But basically, in *Barbican's End* or *Karenza* for instance, it is the atmosphere that makes the book viable. Mind you, this approach can have its drawbacks, in that being conscious that atmosphere alone has its limits, I have often thrown away a possible novel by settling for a shorter version in a short story. Only yesterday a review from the *Manchester Evening News* arrived in the post in which the reviewer picking out the opening story, 'Two Women', from a recent collection, *At the Sea's Edge*, commented ' "Two Women" could well have, by playing on the sinister implications, become a novel in itself.' The idea had just not occurred to me before; now and ever after, maddeningly, thanks to that perceptive reviewer, I shall go on cursing myself for not seeing the obvious truth of his remark! Another might-have-been novel!

So the ups and downs of a writer's life. Like most professional writers, whenever possible I work regular hours, preferably every morning, and in this way find it possible to accomplish quite a reasonable body of work. I write a first draft quickly at what might romantically be termed white-hot speed: then I sit down and rewrite the whole thing, or at the least revise it. Finally I send it off to a regular typist from whom it comes back seemingly virginal and untouched, almost as if written by another hand. Then is the time for one of the most pleasant of all tasks, rather like a painter touching up a finished painting, I suppose – a word here, a correction there, and the final impact, for good or ill, of a completed work.

All this I do in a small wooden hut, originally a garden shed, with windows looking out on a vista of trees and the bubbling tributary of the River Penberth. In the foliage opposite blackbirds and thrushes, robin and chaffinches, above all, the ubiquitous tits, jump about endlessly. Everywhere there is a sense of life and movement, even in a remote valley like ours. It is, I guess, as good a way as almost any other of spending one's life.

III

The Psychological Approach

Life at the Mill House, as autumn progressed relentlessly towards winter, was not entirely physical. When not tending her vegetable garden, prettying her rockery, painting the water wheel, helping Alan to clear out his studio or showing Demelza how to hessian-paper her caravan walls, Jess sometimes found time to develop, or perhaps I should say attempt to develop, her career as a professional psychologist.

I described in *As the Stream Flows By* how after completing her university course with a degree in psychology Jess briefly embarked on a PhD course at Plymouth Polytechnic but eventually gave this up, somewhat disillusioned. Since then she had made several endeavours to make use of her new-found professional skills in the service of the Department of Health or the Cornwall County Council, but it appeared that there were no real openings for psychologists. I felt as strongly as Jess about the absurdity of this lacklustre attitude on the part of local authorities, for if ever there was an area teaming with people in need of psychological treatment it must be Cornwall.

Since it seemed impossible to get anywhere on the official level Jess had decided to set up as a private consultant, and a good deal of our time had been spent looking for suitable premises in Penzance from which she could operate. Rather surprisingly this task also had so far proved impossible, and for the moment she had decided to start her new career by seeing patients out at the Mill House.

First, of course, it was necessary to let prospective patients know of her existence. The simplest thing seemed to be to put a regular advertisement in the local newspaper, *The Cornishman*. After sending this off with a cheque Jess was somewhat piqued to find no advertisement in the next issue – and in the same post an explanation from the advertisement manager stating that it was against the policy of *The Cornishman* to accept such advertisements. There had obviously been some confusion between psychologists, whose British Psychological Society permits advertising under certain conditions, and doctors, whose British Medical Association forbids advertising. After this had been sorted out, the advertisement was put very prominently at the top of the column of personal advertisements ... At least if anyone in the Penzance area was emotionally upset and needing treatment they could hardly fail to know that help was available.

Or so we thought! In fact for several weeks the response to Jess's advertisement was almost negligible. Apart from one client who came through being a friend of a friend, her two out-of-the-blue applications were both a little bizarre. The first was a forever anonymous gentleman who rang up saying could he come and see her the following weekend as during the week he was at sea working as a fisherman. An appointment was made and Jess tidied up her sitting room and sat and waited – and waited – and, alas, waited. It transpired that that was the very day of one of the worst winter gales and for sometime after we were haunted by an uneasy feeling that maybe what would have been her first customer might well have been among the crews of several boats that were sunk off Land's End on that occasion.

The second time there was a real sense of urgency; someone telephoned insisting that he must see Jess that very moment. The trouble was he had no car but he could get a bus to St Buryan and could he walk from there? Since St Buryan is about three miles from our house there seemed no alternative to Jess getting out the car and driving to meet the inquirer and then, after listening to his problems and offering advice, driving him back again. As she had made it a rule to make no charge for a first appointment, the financial success of the enterprise depended on future appointments. Alas, we never heard from that gentleman again.

Despite these somewhat discouraging beginnings Jess was convinced that once she could find a settled room in Penzance where she could hold consultancies more conveniently her new venture would get off the ground – and this, in the event, looked like proving to be so, when she was offered the use of a room in Alexandra Road, one of the main thoroughfares in Penzance. At least the knowledge that she had the use of a room at last enabled her to embark on the important spadework of getting cards printed, writing private letters to local doctors and so forth. (Several local doctors had already privately assured her they would be most happy to make use of the assistance of a trained psychologist.) So gradually Jess was able to feel that there was now a chance of really making use of her three years intensive training at London University.

In another way she had already started doing this by launching a WEA course of lectures on 'An Introduction to Modern Psychotherapy and its Leading Exponents', held every Monday night at the Penzance Public Library. The WEA have a very simple rule about their lectures: if the lecturer can guarantee ten regular attenders, then the lectures can go ahead. If not, they stop after the first meeting! Fortunately there seemed immediate interest in Jess's lectures: at one time she had nearly twenty people on the books, and certainly there were never less than a dozen at the classes. This is hardly surprising really since she was talking on such figures as Freud, Jung, Skinner, Berne, Maslow and many other prominent figures, concluding with the man who had most impressed her (and whose seminar she had attended the previous summer) Carl Rogers, propagator of the idea of client-centred therapy.

Although I felt it tactful to keep well out of the way I soon heard enthusiastically from some of the people attending about the way in which Jess put over her subject, and this made all the more annoying the frustrations put in her way by local official bodies. Indeed the only drawback really about the lecture course was, as Jess found, that people attending became so involved that it was hard to end each session. At least it would have been hard if the Penzance Public Library did not appear to appoint a special kind of time watching official, a very firm lady who came round to put out the lights and lock up always (naturally) at just the most animated point of the evening's discussion. To some extent this problem was alleviated by Jess and several of the pupils adjourning to the nearest pub to carry on talking but it was rather annoying and made Jess long once more for a proper centre of her own – which one day I feel sure she will have.

Although I never attended any of the classes I did finally have a chance of meeting the members as Jess decided to hold the last meeting out at the Mill House, so that at the end of the lecture and discussion she could offer some wine and hospitality as an end-of-term gesture. Many of the people attending were mutual friends, like Judy Emanuel and Dennis Lane, but it was interesting to meet some of the other people, ranging from housewives to nurses, from teachers to social workers. Obviously there is a widening appreciation of the importance of psychology, of understanding ourselves, a trend that can surely do nothing but good. On the evening of the gathering I solved the problem of what to do while the class was in progress. Judy had brought along her husband, the painter John Emanuel, and while the others sat discussing things earnestly in our sitting room, he and I had a meditative drink in the kitchen and talked about some of our own personal problems. Later we joined the others round a blazing fire … altogether a very pleasant evening which, thanks to being free from the strictness of the guardian from Penzance Library, continued gaily until after midnight!

Although one of my weekly jobs was to type out the rather daunting synopses which Jess prepared for each of her lectures, I could not pretend that I was any nearer to a very deep interest in her chosen subject. I was relieved to find that John Emanuel felt very much the same as myself though I have no doubt the psychological explanation of this would be that it was simply a classic case of husbands being jealous of their wives doing their own thing! The truth is that like my son, Stephen, I instinctively shy away from an over-scientific approach to life, from the cut-and-dried patterns which seem to be applied by psychologists and their like. Personally the thing I find interesting about life and about people is not how similar they are, but how different they can be.

The sort of writer who fascinates me – and again, curiously, Stephen, with whom in many other ways I have little in common – is Lyall Watson, author of *Supernature,* followed later by a truly magical book about a year he spent living among the natives of Indonesia. This, I think is because Lyall Watson *has been* a scientist, indeed still is a scientist, but has had the passion (and the humility) to break through the conventional patterns, to begin to grasp that the meanings of life are too mysterious for conventional measurement and analysis. Sad to say, I have got off on the wrong foot with Jess about poor Mr Watson, and his name can hardly be mentioned in our household.

With psychology very much in the air during this pre-Christmas period it was an ironic moment for me to receive a truly textbook anonymous letter. I am used to getting letters out of the blue, but these are usually rather flattering fan letters about my books. Nothing quite like this had ever come my way before, and perhaps it is interesting to quote it in full, tactfully not spelling out some of the most obscene expletives.

Publish this free if you wish. I have read your idiotic book *A Family for all Seasons* only because I am interested in Cornwall. No wonder your family are such idiots with you as a father. Your criminal daughter plays Bongoes, not Bongos* you ignorant goon. If she had inherited *any* brains or been given *any* education she might have played some *solo* instrument in the gutter instead of *begging* for someone else. P.146. It is *not* the correct procedure to drive on the pavement, you ignorant —, it is *illegal*. Trust your useless son to break the law. Pavements are for *pedestrians*. P.122.

---

* Unlike my correspondent, the Oxford English Dictionary finds both spellings acceptable.

Only an ignorant *goon* like you would auction a valuable harp locally instead of sending it to Sotheby's. Don't you know that auctioneers *buy things in* when they don't reach the reserve, you useless ignorant —? Why didn't you *ask* first, you moron? P.152. The reason why idiots ask you for autographs is because only *cretins* and *halfwits* would read books by and about *halfwits*. Even a useless boring — like you might have the sense to realise that. You should be glad *anyone* reads them. *Christ knows why*, they must be gluttons for punishment.

Now your half-witted son has married an American hippy I suppose they will breed loads more — and *quarter-wits* to be a *burden* on the state and be *parasites* like you. P.161. Gillian Tindall is a *respected* author and is *quite right* not to be published by a useless *hack* like you. You are worse than a prostitute as I suppose even *they* give *some* value for money. The only people who *would* publish you are unknown *spivs*. When you *had* some money you only wasted it on a stupid boat and then whined because you were broke. No wonder your wife left you. Why did she come back? P.S. Banks don't *deal* in halfpennies. If I were in the idiot business I would buy six like you. If I were *poor* enough I would buy *twelve*. *Drop Dead* and make this a *really* Happy Christmas. PS. You can't say *hopefully*, you illiterate —.

As what I suppose was meant to be the final insult the letter had been posted in a plain envelope without a stamp, the sender no doubt hoping I would even have to pay for the pleasure of reading his (or her) garbage, but thanks to our pleasantly casual postal service nobody noticed the lack of a stamp. We all read and then re-read this strange epistle with a kind of morbid fascination. At first my reaction had been rather as on a previous occasion many years back when I first read a lurid article in the *People* newspaper attacking me viciously at a time when I was involved with others in an idealistic scheme to go off and start a community in New Zealand, namely just to shrug and forget about it all. On that occasion I was persuaded by Jess and other angry friends not to be so supine; and a good thing, too, as in due course we sued the *People* and received very handsome damages.

In the case of an anonymous letter there is little hope of such redress, but now once again, as other members of the family voiced their growing wrath, I began taking a second and third look at this strange new object in my life. For us all it began to acquire a curious fascination as if we were detectives confronted with a crime, given some clues and now challenged to get some results. The handwriting – well it is more hand*printing* really; nothing much to go on there. Or was there? One perceptive friend picked out the firm way individual letters were formed, the decisive manner 't's' were crossed, little things like that. Another felt the whole style of the letter, dashed off at great heat, suggested perhaps someone under the influence of drink. Personally I did not go along with that – there were too many cold blooded assaults and, though rather clumsily done, attempts to upset people in the family. Perhaps the most useful clues were circumstantial ones. Local knowledge was revealed by one or two other remarks, while all the evidence pointed to the writer being quite well acquainted either with the family as a whole, or with some of its members. Come to think of it that latter point was important: other members of the family were *not* brought in, only myself, Demelza and Stephen.

And so? It *was* rather like a detective case, in many ways, and for quite a while we attempted to exercise our minds. After all surely between quite a crowd of us we could eliminate false clues and centralise upon likely suspects? It proved an interesting psychological exercise, and I must admit I, not least, developed one or two very strong suspicions (difficult ever afterwards to view these unfortunate souls in quite the same way, I am ashamed to say). Then in the end, quite suddenly, the whole thing became boring. Deep down one could only feel pity for the sort of person who could only find fulfilment by venting spleen and filthy epithets from behind the cloak of anonymity. And anyway in the end, precisely because of the secrecy, one was left with a sense of exasperation, since nothing could be discussed, no points could be reported, no mistakes rectified (after all, in all fairness, it is difficult to think of my respectable publishers as 'spivs'!) Yes, that was our feeling at the end of it all. Negative – a sense of nothingness.

And so, on with the more worthwhile business of everyday living. Actually at about the time of the infamous anonymous letter life at the Mill House had been much enlivened for Jess and myself by visits from several old friends. While I had been away in the summer I had been rather sad to hear of the arrival at the Mill – all the way from Australia! – of an old friend who had been an actor with me at the old Studio Theatre, Camborne. By the time I came back he had disappeared back to the other side of the world and we shall probably never meet again.

Fortunately another old friend suddenly descended, not from Australia, but from quite a long way away: the Western Isles of Scotland. This was Donald Swan and his wife Elizabeth, the same Donald who so gaily illustrates the covers of these autobiographical books and who once used to share the Old Vicarage, St Hilary with Jess and me in those dreamy delightful poverty-stricken days when Stephen was three, Demelza had recently been born and Genevieve was just about on the way. Donald is a year younger than I, which I think I can fairly claim still makes us contemporaries, and I was pleased to see him looking as well as ever. Both he and Elizabeth, I fancy, have always rather regretted leaving Cornwall, and though they have a thriving pottery business at Millport up on the Isle of Cumbrae and live in a comfortable rambling old converted manse I get the strong feeling that all that Scottish wild beauty of lochs and mountains do not quite compensate for the loss of that easy-going companionship that was so much a part of their life down in Cornwall. Since Elizabeth is, anyway, Cornish-born, and their children are now practically grown up, I have a shrewd suspicion that perhaps it won't be long before we welcome these particular 'Swans' back to their old haunts.

Mind you, as is the case with so many former inhabitants who revisit Cornwall fleetingly, Donald and Elizabeth probably get a heightened and slightly unreal picture of life down here. As Donald said, in a bewildered sort of way, every time they walked down Fore Street in St Ives it seemed they were stopped every few minutes and greeted warmly by one old friend or another. I can remember the same sort of experience when I first returned to St Ives, and it is very heady. For a while one feels the centre of the universe – where of course in harsh everyday life terms this sort of bonhomie soon cools down to a mere normal level. All the same. Cornwall does have something ... doesn't it, Donald and Liz?

Someone I had not actually met before, but who it turned out was confronting the same sort of heart-tugs, called in one day: Ander Gunn, the photographer. For many years he and his family had lived down in North Cornwall, at St Just, and while there he had produced many stunning photographs that captured the Cornish scene more vividly than almost anyone else, and it was over the use of some of his photographs for a forthcoming book that I had begun corresponding. Recently, in the inevitable struggle to make ends meet, Ander Gunn had gone to work for Yorkshire Television, and his visit now was while on a fleeting visit home. He was due back in Leeds the next day, but obviously, he wasn't at all happy at going northwards. He and Jess and I had a fascinating discussion about this eternal problem. His children, like ours, having been brought up in Cornwall, now have it in their blood and don't want to go away; in fact one is still living down here.

Even more unfortunate from his point of view his wife had been so horrified with the dour life of Yorkshire that she had found herself unable to live up there, and was now installed permanently back in their St Just home to which, one couldn't help feeling, it wouldn't be long before Ander also returned! Certainly his stories of the harshness and dourness of Leeds – 'Is it true that Leeds is the nearest thing to Hell on earth?' one famous writer once commented – made one grateful for living in our world of cliffs and sandy beaches, of wild moorlands and twisting lanes, of a place full of space and sky and sea and wonder.

Among our visitors at this period were two more recent

acquaintances – in fact very recent: Bob and Uni, comrades on our last summer cruise on *Sanu*, when we brought her round from Le Grau-du-Roi in France via the Balearic Isles and the Straits of Gibraltar to her present home in Vilamoura, Portugal. Bob was the first to come; with his instinctive interest in mechanical things he was soon deep in the technical problems of the water wheel and various other machines which always seem to lie around the Mill House. As I explained in *As the Stream Flows By*, Bob had done a wonderful job keeping our old Kelvin diesel going during *Sanu*'s cruise; indeed he has joined Stephen and Llewellyn in the hall of fame as one of our Official Diesel Engineers.

While the other two had momentarily rather lost contact with the boat Bob was still full of warm memories, and we had some enjoyable reminiscences of our days abroad – especially the last couple of weeks when with just Bob, his girl friend Rosie, and Uni as crew we took *Sanu* 400 miles out of the Med and up the Portugal coast. During this time we had a traumatic stop at Gibraltar where the medical officer thought Rosie had typhoid and whisked her off to hospital! Fortunately we had survived all that but I hadn't seen Bob since we parted at Vilamoura and he now told me how he and Rosie had hitched all over Portugal before returning home.

Now back in London, Bob was running a public address system for the use of rock bands in discos and folk clubs, while in his spare time constantly doing up old cars and fiddling about with engines and transformers and what not. I always look upon engineering experts like Bob with a certain awe, being completely useless in this field myself, but I suppose it is all relative and they probably marvel at my casual easiness with words.

At any rate we were very glad to see Bob, and then a little later Uni – the latter, of course, no stranger to Cornwall or our house, as he had spent some years around Penzance and was a close friend of both Martin and Stephen. Uni had been the great comedian of our boat trips, always up to one lark or another, vying with me in bad-punning and constantly having us in fits of laughter. At the same time he had been most helpful practically, since he was a trained carpenter ... like many others before him he had left a personal legacy aboard *Sanu,* in his case in the form of a new sampson post and some repairs to the transom.

Like Bob I think Uni had been quite profoundly affected by the experience of the trip: if nothing else it had given him itchy feet – indeed when we left Vilamoura he had stayed on a few weeks to see if perhaps he could pick up a boat heading for the West Indies, but without luck. Even now, I could sense, he was ready to jump at some similar chance, even though in the meantime mundanely he was having to eke out a living in London doing odd repair jobs by day, and a round of folk clubs in the evenings. Wherever he went Uni took with him his battered little violin case, and now, while he was staying up in the chalet with Stephen he was forever bringing it out and joining with Stephen, and Genny and Melza, if they were down, in a good old jam session.

Speaking of jam sessions, Demelza had recently experienced another step forward in her musical career, or so we hoped. While out in Minorca she had bumped into Mike Oldfield, for whom she had already done some recording, and perhaps this had led to Mike reminding his drummer, Pierre, about Demelza's prowess as a bongo-player. At any rate while still away Demelza had been sent a telegram inviting her to go on a tour with a new band Pierre had formed called The Gong. Unfortunately by the time she returned to England the band had embarked on their tour, but hearing she was back, Pierre invited her to come and play with them at one of their last performances of their tour, at the Venue, in Victoria, London. Alas, I was not present but we heard from Genevieve that the evening was a great personal triumph for Demelza whose playing was so brilliant that Pierre insisted on her doing a solo – while after the performance she was surrounded by autograph hunters! What with a big champagne party in the dressing room afterwards Demelza was entitled to feel on the top of the world – especially as Pierre insisted on her staying with the band and playing Birmingham the following night in their final concert.

Meanwhile, back at the Mill House, we had noticed that not only Demelza but Genny too now had greatly improved musically (she plays the tenor saxophone) and when they joined in with Stephen on the piano, often in our little hallway, it sounded like very professional music indeed. Why on earth didn't they go ahead and form a band of their own, a Val Baker band? It seemed, and seems, a not unreasonable idea ... perhaps one day we shall see it in practice. In the meantime Jess and I were happy enough to settle back in our old people's chairs in the sitting room and listen to these free concerts, the band often augmented by friends such as Uni and Uffy, a brilliant guitar player, or perhaps like Chrissie Quayle, another saxophonist, with whom Genevieve once hitched across America. Oh, yes, there's never a dull moment, musically, at the Mill House!

Other moments, though, can be dull – this is the price one pays for living deep in the countryside, I suppose. Actually this was a problem that was beginning to bother Jess and me more than a little, and still does. After a life of considerable social activity, recent years had seen a steady withdrawal into a more remote life – for me, obviously more than Jess, for she did have her three years at university. However for nearly a year now Jess, like myself, had been spending all her time at the Mill House, and though periodically we had visits from children and friends, for much of the time now we were entirely alone. Was this exactly what we wanted for the remainder of our life?

At first it was something we would talk about airily, rather unreally, but as time went by I think we both began to appreciate that sooner or later it was likely to become more than a merely academic question. At the time of writing everything seems still unresolved. If we were younger I feel sure, we would have organised ourselves and some friends and gone off on *Sanu* on a voyage round the world, something like that. Rightly or wrongly I feel I am a little over the hump for such a responsibility, and anyway recently I have become slightly haunted by forebodings that after fourteen relatively magical years with *Sanu* – lots of traumas, but no fatalities –

our luck must surely be heading for that inevitable moment when it just might run out (for the first time in my life, strangely, I was feeling quite apprehensive about our forthcoming and final trip back from Portugal to Cornwall).

And so, if not a solution through *Sanu*, what else? One answer for Jess could be taking a job in London, in psychology, which undoubtedly she would find interesting and stimulating. However, I don't think even she is all that keen on returning to the dust and rat race of London. The alternative that appeals to her equally is one that possibly, over a period, I may somehow manage to encompass. It is after the style of *Sanu* – travel. But travel in a more orthodox fashion, principally in order to see all those wonderful places we have never seen. There are problems about it all of course – fortunately neither of us has the least wish to visit India, or for that matter Japan, but Jess does hanker after seeing China, which I don't: on the other hand we would both love to travel across Russia, preferably via the Trans-Siberian Railway. Then there is South America – that sounds an exciting new world indeed.

Will we ever do anything about it? As with most things in our family life I am inclined to think the final answer may come in the form of some outside influence. Perhaps I will get a commission for a book – perhaps Jess will get the chance to visit some psychology foundation – perhaps, well, there are all kinds of perhaps's! One way or another I have a sneaking feeling that even if *Sanu* looks likely to settle for a while back in her original home of Cornish waters, her owners might nevertheless still keep travelling.

IV

Gales to Remember

In November, when it still seemed only yesterday we were all lying basking in the sun on that marvellous little island of Esplanadar, off Formentera in the Balearic Isles, possibly one of the most romantic anchorages we have ever found aboard *Sanu*, suddenly the dreaded phrase began to be bandied around on the radio: 'Only thirty more shopping days to Christmas' and then soon, 'Only twenty shopping days to Christmas'. Every year I keep lying in wait to make sure I won't be caught napping by this sly onslaught of the inevitable festive season, and every year somehow I find myself surprised.

On this occasion, however, we were in for surprises of a rather more violent nature before we reached the comparative haven of Christmas time. While we had been away in the summer Cornwall had experienced one of its worst gales in history at the time of the ill-fated Fastnet race, upon which inquests were still being held. Only the other night we had watched spell-bound as a television programme recreated the horrors of that night – horrors doubly poignant to us because of our own knowledge of the sea, and what it can do to mere human beings. At least we had been fortunate enough not to be around at the time, we thought ... I suppose, too, we were inclined to think that maybe Cornwall had therefore *had* its bad bout of weather at least for the current year.

Not a bit of it. One Friday night – I can remember it well for it was indeed the night of Jess's farewell gathering of her psychology students – the air began to vibrate from an ominous whining and whistling of the wind. Down in our valley wind is not usually much of a problem since we are protected on two sides by high rising ground, while long stretches of tall elm trees fill up most of the other space. However, we *are* narrowly open at each end in the direction along which our river flows, approximately north-east and south-west.

On this particular evening the wind must have been blowing from the south-west at just such an angle as to send it blasting up our little valley. At first, of course, ensconced in our cosy sitting room, drinking wine and chatting animatedly, we hardly paid much attention to the outside weather, beyond subconsciously noting an occasional sudden boom of wind and distant noise of thunder. Only when everyone began departing and I opened the outside door and caught the strong gusts of wind in my face did it begin to dawn upon me that we might be in for a rough night. Ah well, I told myself comfortingly, it's always worse on top than down here.

This might well be true, but on this occasion, for a change, it was going to be almost as bad down in our 'protected' valley as in the 'unprotected' up there. Jess and I went to bed about one o'clock and for a while things did not seem too bad, perhaps we even dozed off ... Suddenly we were both awoken by a definite and ominous increase in the whistling and whining of the wind. Outside we could hear the tall trees being positively battered about, and for the first time a chill of worry, even fear, came over us.

Thank goodness we couldn't help thinking, Demelza and Genny were away and not sleeping in their caravan, surrounded by tall trees, some of them nearly 100 feet high, and several suspected of having contracted Dutch elm disease. But what about Stephen and Gina, and their little baby Amira and young Paris living in the chalet higher up – were they going to be safe?

At one stage I took a quick look out: there was a high moon riding in the sky, now and then obliterated by clouds that seemed positively to be racing hither and thither. Illuminated by the moonlight the chalet looked solid enough, and looking across the lawn I could see that as yet no trees had fallen on the caravan. Everything seemed all right; and yet there was something in the air, some menace about the blowing of the wind that left me with a great feeling of unease. I went back to bed and Jess and I pulled the bedclothes over our heads and tried to sleep, but it was an uneasy night.

In the morning we found that our unease was not without cause. Reports were coming through on the radio of freak storms and gales all over England, and particularly affecting the West Country. Gusts had been recorded at Land's End of up to 120 miles per hour.

'Do you realise,' Jess said in some awe, 'at sea that would be *Force 12*?' (Force 12, by the way, which is practically unheard of normally, is worse than a gale, worse than a storm, even worse than a cyclone.) From all accounts, judging by the preliminary news flashes, there had been considerable damage – roofs blown off, walls down, streets flooded, and of course, inevitably, many dramas at sea.

So much for the world news. Now it was time to step outside and see what the gales had done to our little patch of green and pleasant land. The alarming answer was – quite a lot.

The first thing we saw were several patches of slates blown clean off the main cottage roof, exposing the bare timbers beneath. Well, we had had that sort of thing before; it could soon be put right by a competent local builder we knew. Ah, now, but what had happened over there, beyond that clump of tall bamboos, in that far corner? What indeed? Poor Alan's proud new building, the last thing one would have imagined to be caught by the wind for it appeared completely sheltered, that had suffered more than anywhere. Somehow the wind had got under the roofing felt and relentlessly torn most of it off exposing practically the whole area of twenty by thirty feet. Worse still, once the felt was gone, exposing the roofing section, the wind had been so strong that it had literally lifted up an entire section and sent it crashing down into the interior. There it lay now across the brightly polished floor, everywhere dripping with water and covered with dirt and leaves, leaving in the roof a yawning gap eight by ten feet wide, through which the rain was even now beginning to pour.

Thoroughly alarmed, for secretly we had always felt confident of being comparatively sheltered in all sorts of weather, Jess and I tramped around. Rather to our surprise Stephen's chalet appeared to have survived relatively intact, apart from a broken television aerial and one or two dents in his hall roofing. Furthermore Demelza's caravan, despite its canopy of trees which on the previous night had seemed to be alive as they swayed wildly in all directions, was the least disturbed of all. Coming nearer to the house however, we soon found further quite serious damage, this time to the old workshop in the front garden which some years before we had converted into a pottery. Here most of the corrugated roofing had been ripped away by the winds, many of the wooden struts below broken, so that everywhere inside was exposed to the elements including two valuable kilns. Worst of all the wind had been so strong that in tearing off the roofing at one corner it had also bulldozed down most of the outside south wall, which now lay in crumbled ruins on the lawn.

When we finally sat down in our kitchen Jess and I realised that this was very much a case for the insurance company. When we tried telephoning them the number was constantly engaged – we did not appreciate it at the time but that night had witnessed one of the worst natural disasters in West Cornwall for many a long year. Eventually we managed to get through and the insurance company promised to send us a claim form. Since it was obvious from what we told them that the damage was going to run into some hundreds of pounds they explained that they would need to send an assessor over, so we begged them to do this as soon as possible ... and sat down to wait.

Unbelievably and ironically, while we were sitting and waiting, the elements played their second joke. Only six days after the first storm West Cornwall was struck by another, and in some ways worse than the first. Certainly, as we found one quick tour of the district next day, the damage was quite horrific. One farm complex through which we always passed on our journey to Land's End had not a single roof left standing; everything was in a state of disarray.

So, for that matter, were we – all over again. More damage to Alan's building, more to the pottery, more slates off our own roof – and, new and much more upsetting to Jess, our beloved new greenhouse, high up on the side of the hill, was completely shattered, a tangled mass of wreckage. Not only was the glass broken into smithereens but the actual aluminium frame all twisted and tangled, as if it had been caught in an explosion.

By coincidence that same day the assessor made his arrival, which was fortunate from our point of view as he was able to see the damage while still fresh. He took a pitying look around the smashed greenhouse, (and also I may add the pathetic remains of the little hut I had not long ago so proudly built) and said pithily:

'Well, *that's* a write-off for a start.'

The assessor spent a considerable time going around the whole property and quickly approved all our claims for damages. At the same time he complained that we were under-insured.

'I've been trying to work out a valuation,' he explained and went on to give a rather astronomical figure which I suppose was some comfort to us – although as he himself pointed out house prices had taken off like a rocket and bore very little resemblance any more to reality. Indeed, as an example, high as was the value of our house, if we were disposed to sell it we would undoubtedly need every penny with which to buy any property of comparable attraction.

And so, it would seem, the moral is – don't sell. The fact is anyway, I think, Jess and I feel that we have come to the end of the road so far as house selling comes. In our time we have bought and sold about ten houses (rather fewer than I would have imagined until I did a count). Each experience has been quite exciting, yet I always had the feeling when we moved to the Mill House that perhaps now, as we get older, we would put our roots down more finally. Circumstances may always alter, of course – we may be off round the world in a few weeks time, who knows? – but there is somewhere this feeling of having found a reasonably permanent haven. With about three acres of rambling land it does have the advantage of providing space enough for our growing brood to gather around, spending holidays with us, or staying in a caravan or camping out – nice to have a family centre!

During our two rather alarming December gales, along with many other fascinated local people, we ventured out to one or two exposed points like Logan Rock and Land's End in order to see how things were out at sea. Things, to put it succinctly, were absolutely fearful. Charlie Roff, who used to be a lifeguard at Porthcurno, said that he had never known such huge waves in all his time there – and we saw the same great waves crashing up the long wide beach at Sennen. I have noticed before that the sands at Sennen are constantly changed by the varying tides – which incidentally are creeping further inland all the time, encroaching steadily upon the sand-dune foothills. Recently the local Friends of the Earth have been organising special planting sessions at which groups of volunteers put down rows and rows of sand grass in an attempt to halt the erosion.

I have become very fond of Sennen beach in recent years partly because it is our nearest of any size, but also, I think, because it can offer such a variety of entertainments. First, it is one of the biggest and best surfing beaches not only in Cornwall but in Britain, attracting professional surfers from all over the world. I think I am right in saying that a Sennen girl surfer won the current British surf championships for ladies, and that several local men surfers invariably win their way into the finals. Because it is the only beach in Cornwall that directly faces the oncoming western Atlantic waves there is seldom a day when surfing is not possible at Sennen and I can literally count on the fingers of one hand the number of times I have been there in the past few years without there being at least half a dozen rubber-suited surfers out there waiting for 'the big one'.

In my surfing days we simply used the old-fashioned boards; now it is either malibu boards, the kind of solid objects on which the surfer first kneels and then, once he is sure he has caught a wave, stands – or, as is popular at

Sennen, surfing canoes, in which the rider is strapped into an unsinkable kayak canoe.

I should imagine surf canoeing is very exciting indeed, though the moment of capsizing always looks pretty hair-raising. However they go about it – whether literally hand-surfing without a board at all (quite an art), surfing on the small boards or on malibus, or surfing canoeing – I am sure that the lads and girls at Sennen experience an exhilaration and even ecstasy which their city fellows might well envy them. I know I do.

Surfing, however is not the only attraction at Sennen beach, or rather Whitesands Bay to give it its proper name. For quite a while hang-gliding became a popular sport, and one can easily understand why looking up at the long line of cliff land surmounting the gently undulating sand dunes. Unlike much of the grim Cornish coast, with rocks waiting below with angry bared fangs, along Sennen beach there are large areas of soft sands and so that one imagines even if a hang-glider plummeted directly downwards the fall would be reasonably cushioned. At least I assume so, as on the several occasions I have watched hang-gliding this seemed almost inevitably to be the process: first a long laborious period down on the beach while the hang-glider was strapped into his complicated harness, then an even more laborious climb carrying all this equipment on the back up the slippery sand slopes to the very peak. There the hang gliders would stand sometimes two or three in a line, waiting for the right puff of wind ('thermal' I believe is the correct technical term).

Often, with the bright sunshine outlining the poised figures it made quite a dramatic sight – one indeed that gave rise to higher expectations than seemed to be fulfilled. Whenever I watched what happened was this: at last the requisite puff of air arrived and with a series of rather ugly movements the hang-glider waddled rather like a fat duck towards the edge and suddenly launched himself off into the vast space – hanging there for perhaps four or five seconds of agonised uncertainty before, alas, the thermal proved insufficient to carry his weight and he began tumbling towards the ground ... usually being saved from any serious injury by a

combination of the drag effect of the winds, the comparative
short distance, and the softness of the sand. Nevertheless I
assume there must have been one or two fairly serious
accidents for in recent times hang-gliders have been noticeable
by their absence at Sennen.

Never mind, our local beach can offer still other attractions.
Dogs, for instance: it is a beach that seems to draw dogs as
magnetically as it draws surfers and swimmers. Dogs of all
kinds, small ones and large, Alsatians and pekes, poodles and
greyhounds, and of course mongrels like our own dear Roxy,
whose idea of heaven is racing off across that vast sea of sand,
pretending to chase seagulls or maybe a piece of flotsam we
have thrown. It is a glorious place for dogs indeed, where they
can be free of all those pettifogging restrictions quite
reasonably imposed in towns, and just enjoy the elements.

The elements themselves, of course, are part of the
entertainment at Sennen, for seldom a day passes there
without either the sea or the sky or both combining to produce
the most astounding visual effects. I can remember several
times crossing Whitesands Bay in *Sanu* in the old days, and my
memory is that *from the sea* the bay itself does not look of
startling interest: Cape Cornwall or Land's End and its
Longships Lighthouse, which bound the bay at either end, are
another matter altogether, formidable sights to anyone at sea
especially if, as we sometimes did, you found yourselves a little
too close for comfort. However, when one is standing on the
beach itself the atmosphere seems totally different; there is a
strong sense of wonder and awe as one looks out upon the long
line of relentless white breakers smashing over the tiny
harbour wall close by one of England's most westerly lifeboat
stations with its runway pointing out into a small patch of safe
water surrounded by fearsome rocks.

Watching the waves alone can occupy half an hour; there is
an absolute fascination both in their uniformity and in the
constant look-out for the odd rogue wave, the one bigger than
usual which suddenly smashes down and comes racing up the
beach perhaps for a hundred feet further inland than the
previous wave.

Another reason for watching the waves closely, apart from

the excitement of glimpsing one of the surfers catching the wave and zooming in like some young god of olden times is the strong possibility of spotting a dark shape somewhere which is not a human being, but one of the charming and friendly seals which hang around that part of the coast. Sometimes it is difficult to be sure whether the shape is a seal or the more rare dolphin, but both are equally mischievous and entertaining.

I once watched a particular seal start at one end of the beach and shuffle his way right across until he had reached a group of surfers, there to play around on the outskirts of their activities, showing no fear whatsoever. Probably readers have heard tales of 'Beaky', the famous dolphin with a great liking for the Cornish coast – he has been a frequent visitor to Sennen Cove, of course, and there are others like him. What delightful creatures are the dolphins and seals, like playful children.

Then, too, there are other groups, like basking sharks that come in quite close to the shore; they are not so playful but seem to move in unison, rather like a gang. One cannot help wondering what they make of this strange man-impinging world ahead of them – no wonder, reading the newspapers with their horrific images of insanity at large, that the creatures of the deep so often turn and disappear out to sea again!

In the summertime, of course, Sennen, like most other beaches in Cornwall, can become rather impossibly crowded. To complain about this could be regarded as a selfish outlook, but it is simply a truism and no way round it. Eventually the whole thing will become such a problem that it might well almost reach the stage described in a play I once wrote for radio in which I envisaged the conditions at St Ives becoming such that visitors in their cars are guided down to the harbour where they take up appropriate positions, finding themselves surrounded completely by a six foot high concrete wall, but being given periscopes through which they can look out upon the sea and sights!

This hasn't quite happened yet in Cornwall, but there is every indication that it may. I don't know what the answer is and neither apparently does anyone else. Foreign travel, which it was assumed would remove large sections of the holiday population from British resorts, has been hit by inflation, and the impression I get is that more people are choosing Cornwall for their holidays than ever before. Frankly, while the problem *is* a problem, to me it seems to be of such short duration that it is up to us 'locals' to shoulder it manfully, make visitors at home as much as possible – and then, breathing a sigh of relief, enjoy our great privilege of Cornwall in the winter, which can be so much more exciting and exhilarating even than the summer.

Sadly, exciting and exhilarating are hardly the adjectives that could be applied to some of the coastal disasters of that somewhat exceptional December. Although in Cornwall we are only too familiar with local sea disasters I think everyone was shocked by a whole series of sinkings of boats, sometimes quite close to shore, along with inevitable loss of life. There is no point in cataloguing them here, except perhaps to consider one rather significant one, the loss of the Scottish fishing boat *Bounteous* which, like many other Scottish boats, had recently acquired the habit during the winter months of coming down to fish in Cornish waters.

This influx of Scottish fishing boats, and for that matter boats from the East Coast, from Lowestoft and Hull, has hardly been popular among the Cornish fishermen – and not without good reason, for the bigger up-country boats with their heavy nets were reputed to be rapidly denuding the Cornish fishing grounds. The whole thing, indeed, had recently accelerated as there had also arrived on the scene packs of large Russian and East German trawlers and refrigerated carriers whose captains were only too happy to buy catches direct from the boatmen.

Yet despite all these disagreements and alarums, whenever disaster hits at sea, down in Cornwall as I am sure anywhere else, the heartwarming truth is that instinctively and courageously fishermen of all kinds (and of course lifeboatmen and coastguards and others) close ranks to come to the rescue. At such times it is men against the sea, not Scottish fishermen versus Cornish fishermen, and the only sad thing is that it should need a tragedy to bring about such co-operation. I suppose, upon reflection, exactly the same can be said in the international sphere – if this world was suddenly confronted with some disaster from outer space we can be sure that the Russians and the Americans, the Chinese and the British, the Germans, the French, the Italians – yes, and the Israelis and the Arabs – would soon be working side by side for the same cause.

Soon after the *Bounteous* disaster, I happened to be in Newlyn so I parked the car and took one of my favourite walks out along the North Pier. I had forgotten in the meantime that with the aid of a much delayed grant the Newlyn Harbour Commissioners had at long last built a whole new series of quays: now, seeing the work almost finished I realised what a very large and important fishing port Newlyn had become. Looking around the forest of masts my heart stirred as always – even though for a moment, forgetting what had happened a couple of years back, I started searching for that dear old sister boat of *Sanu, Karenza* (sadly, lost at sea after a fire). Nevertheless what I saw made a grand sight.

Here was a true working fishing port, something to be proud of in a county too much tainted by the artificiality of tourism. So long as Cornwall has places like Newlyn and Falmouth, Mevagissey and Fowey, as well as those wilder and more elemental vistas of Land's End, Cape Cornwall, the Lizard, Tintagel, the Scillies, so long as there are weird lonely places like Carn Euny and Ding-Dong and Carn Brea, haunted hills like Trencrom and Brown Willy, and the white-tipped clay pits of St Austell – in short, so long as the true, natural and non-plastic aspects of the county remain firmly rooted in reality, then indeed Cornwall will remain what I once called it in another book 'the timeless land'.

V

Nostalgia at Christmas

After the whirling winds and battering storms of the
beginning of December Christmas arrived at the Mill House
almost calmly. This was one of those years when not all the
family could be together – as some compensation there was
the exciting prospect that over the New Year holiday the
entire family, parents, children and grandchildren, would be
assembled for the first time ever. That was something to look
forward to indeed! In the meantime Jess and I were able to
prepare in a more relaxed way than usual for the Christmas
period. First the tree – £5 for a rather miserable specimen
which was all we could find in Penzance (oh for those golden
days when the boys would creep out in the night to a distant
common in mid-Cornwall and come back bearing some eight-
foot monster!). Next the decorations – what seemed miles of
cables and bulbs and flashing lights which were draped all
round the sitting room. Then balloons and fancy crackers and
bowls of nuts and fruits and sweets dotted about the old Welsh
dresser and the long low pinewood table. Looking around one
evening at Jess and Genny and Melza and Gina clambering
around – not forgetting Paris, gravely attempting to fix
Christmas cards on to the door with a hammer – I could not
help thinking, surely 'I have been here before'! How many
Christmases had Jess and I carried through in how many
places? At Peter's Cottage on the edge of the cliffs at Land's
End, in that gracious long sitting room of the Old Vicarage at
St Hilary, in the old wood panelled sitting room at the
Elizabethan house we once rented at Mersham, Kent – then
the time in London, when we leased a Georgian terrace house
in Drayton Gardens, Fulham; and above all, in that marvellous

long low downstairs room at St Christopher's, where so many Christmases were held to the sound of huge Atlantic waves booming on the outside door, all boarded up with four-inch thick planks, and probably half-covered with sandbanks washed up by the angry sea ... later at the Old Sawmills at Fowey, where in some ways we had had our cosiest Christmases of all, knowing that we were literally a mile from any other human habitation, sometimes opening our window in the early evening and looking out over a breathtaking vista of the lagoon and beyond the river bank the swirling waters of the River Fowey on an incoming tide – the whole view shimmering with a slight mist of crisp winter.

And now, how many years here at the Mill House? This must be our seventh Christmas, and I must say they had all been very enjoyable, partly because of our warm enveloping sitting room with its bright log fire, a focal point. This year was to prove no exception; when the great day came there were seven of us – Jess and myself, Demelza and Genevieve, Stephen and Gina, and Martin over from his room in Penzance – plus, of course the two grandchildren, Stephen and Gina's four-year-old Paris and one-year-old Amira. In many ways it was a convenient number for sitting at our round table, and spreading ourselves before the big fire afterwards.

As ever we planned the day to include a ritual walk through the fields over to Logan Rock before a mid-day drink, but some softness seems to be entering into the Val Baker family ... though it wasn't particularly cold, nobody seemed very enthusiastic about the walking part of the occasion and everyone opted for making the journey in Martin's old Austin Cambridge.

At the last minute, prodded by some ancient sense of duty maybe, or perhaps because I am a great ritualist I decided that *I* at least would make the walk. The real reason was more likely to prove to myself that despite my weak leg I could still manage a mile on the flat through the woods. That was okay, but the last few hundred yards up the steep hill to the Logan Rock were pretty shattering. Still there was a satisfying sense of achievement once we were in the pub, and just time for a

quick celebratory drink before driving back for our Christmas
lunch.

Over that Christmas I think my most overwhelming feeling
was indeed a persistent impression of *déjà vu* – handing out the
presents from the tree, reading out messages from absent
daughters and sons-in-law, sitting around bloated over-fed,
perhaps relaxing with a game round the fire or some later
television programme – as one gets older it is all so familiar, so
endless, inevitably there is a great sense of weariness. But not,
of course – thank goodness – for the very young. It was
delightful to watch the blond head of little Paris, his eyes
bright and gleaming, and the first cautious crawls around the
golden-coloured carpet of the youngest member of our ever
growing family, little Amira.

And a growing family it was indeed. That fact became
impressively obvious a week later when there assembled at the
Mill House: 2 parents, 4 daughters, 2 sons, 2 sons-in-law, 1
daughter-in-law, and 5 grandchildren – a grand total of 16, 11
adults and 5 small children (it would have been 17 were it not
that Emmy, Gill's spastic daughter, was now in a home where
she was so happy and settled that it would have been pointless
to have her for an occasion which, alas, she could not have
comprehended).

There was certainly about the occasion a sense of history to
which our historian, Martin, was quick to respond. In one of
my earlier books, *How to be a Parent*, there is a frontispiece
picture done in the Victorian style, showing a family group,
Jess and I seated with the older children grouped around us,
'baby' Genevieve on Jess's knee, and it has always been
Martin's ambition to repeat this photograph in exact detail
with the now adult specimens. Here was his golden
opportunity and he prevailed on Charlie Roff, who was
setting up as a photographer, to come out on the Sunday
before New Year's Eve and take such a photograph.

In the event, gathering together such a conglomeration of
people of all ages, sizes and states of mind proved such a
cumbersome process that it must have been a good two hours
before at last we were all out on the lawn, bathed in bright
sunlight, attempting to pose for a rather harassed Charlie. As

one might have guessed it turned out to be one of those rather doomed occasions and Charlie had to shoot the film more in hope than confidence. Still the actual experience was very amusing, what with all the machinations necessary in order to repeat the exact layout of the original photograph. In the end we did manage a very faithful reproduction with a 5ft 4ins Genevieve spread over Jess's lap, and a 5ft 7ins Demelza half balanced on my knee. It was all rather hilarious – and even more so when, having completed one official photo, we naturally wanted to have another one done including all the later acquisitions, like sons-in-law, daughter-in-law and tiny mites of grandchildren.

Alas, when finally Charlie brought round the prints, something very strange had happened. The group was recognisable, even interesting, but the lighting seemed all awry, with black being blacker than usual, and white very stark, and over everything a strange brooding atmosphere that could only really be called 'spooky'. Charlie was as disappointed as the rest of us. What's more he couldn't really understand it, as he had some earlier snapshots taken on the same reel which had printed perfectly. It did seem altogether rather strange, and to me a little ominous – or perhaps I should say omen-nous. Certainly it suggested we were unlikely ever to manage to reproduce that early photograph, and perhaps Martin is wrong to press the point. Leave the past to the past, enjoy the present in the present, worry about the future when it comes. Hark who is talking – one who does all the opposite!

Photographs apart, our New Year Reunion was a great occasion. Not so much for any one event, but for a week of what can indeed be called intensive family living. The Mill House is hardly more than an ordinary Cornish cottage, with 2 bedrooms and 1 smaller one tacked on round the back. Fortunately Demelza and Genny had their caravan and Stephen and Gina the chalet, but all the rest had to sleep in the main house, which meant Jane and Rick and their son Ben and their new daughter Lamorna all in one spare bedroom, and Gill and Alan and their daughter Amber in the other.

That all worked out quite bearably. Mealtimes were another matter. At least Martin was back sleeping in Penzance, but he came out several times for meals of course. Sometimes a gathering of 11 adults and 7 children proved too much even for our famous round table, and we ended up by putting down a small side table for Ben, Paris and Amber, thus easing the congestion. Jess and the girls, or Alan or I, took turns in cooking, but even so it was pretty hectic – though rather marvellous at the penultimate moment when some triumphant cook served up steaming paella, or a great spicy curry (not for me, alas). Plus, of course, endless bottles of Italian wines, some of which I had managed to acquire locally from an enterprising little firm who had set up business, of all places, from a remote cottage on the side of Trencrom Hill – others which the girls had brought with them down from London.

It would have been most unnatural if sometimes, sitting around our New Year Reunion Table, Jess and I had not allowed our minds to wander back across the long years of our family life – goodness, our 31st wedding anniversary was due in four weeks' time! I shall never cease to marvel at the ramifications of this, one of our oldest, most persistently criticised and yet surviving institutions. Even though family life is more under attack now than at almost any other period in history – even though Jess herself, as a psychologist and a political philosopher, intellectually disapproves of the whole set up – what fascinates me is the tenacious way in which the intricate structure persists. Only now as I am writing this paragraph Stephen has just popped in to tell me of two friends of his who, finally faced with the fact that they would be unable ever to have children of their own, have just adopted a three-month-old baby.

'They must be mad. They won't be able to travel like they used to, they'll have to find baby sitters, their life won't be their own ...'

There of course, speaks a proud father of two! I doubt if he would exactly welcome a return to the comparative barren days of childlessness. This, I suppose, is one of the vital points underlying the great family survival. With our children we are making our own images, continuing the line, defying, if you like the Great Reaper himself. (I use the capital letters not out of deference to some mystic deity in which I have no belief but simply in acknowledgement that the world is a more mysterious place than I shall ever comprehend.)

Certainly now, during that rather momentous New Year week when our enlarged family were together for the very first time I did find myself marvelling at all the weather changes that had taken place since that far-off day when we all gravely poised for our Victorian style photograph. Some, I suppose, have changed more than others. Martin, at thirty-five the eldest, looks now very much as he did in that early photograph: handsome, curiously determined, somewhat withdrawn – a loner in life, though curiously someone who has always been surprisingly sociable with a wide circle of friends. Much lower down the age scale, Demelza, too, has not altered greatly, remaining to this day nervous and excitable, quick in triumph and disaster, forever burning with an unquenchable flame of life – exasperating, yet somehow indelibly marking her image on those around her. Gill and Jane have both in different ways greatly matured so that although now and then there are reminders of childhood traumas (especially their own sisterly feuds), in life itself I find them much more adult and interesting: both married and with children they also both have talents they are fulfilling – Gill in her work in pottery and decorations, Jane rather more particularly in her steady climb in the BBC hierarchy where she is now an official editor, working on such programmes as *The World About Us*.

Stephen, too, has plunged into the matrimonial and family pool, and has yet managed miraculously to present a determined capacity to enjoy the everyday things of life without thinking too much about the future (though perhaps this is too dangerous a prediction about a Scorpio whose every action usually is secretly foreplanned).

Perhaps the most changed of all is the youngest, Genevieve. Armed with that stubbornness which is the burden of every Taurus she has persistently shifted her life style from the original golden world of a stunning and lush teenage beauty through the vagaries of hippy life and flower power into a more sensitive world of myths and legends, magic and marvels; travelling, indeed, far more extensively than any other member of the family – to France, to Italy, to Greece, to India, to Nepal, to the USA, to Mexico – but somehow, despite her travelling failing to find her karma, and left searching, thinner and finer-featured, for something she may never find.

Ah, children! How shall we ever really know them when they hardly know themselves? Just as we also do not really know ourselves. Jess and I – in thirty years what has happened to us, indeed? So many things, many recorded in my books, many unrecorded not because they are too personal, but because other people might have been involved or hurt. Apparently we are generally regarded as an open couple, if you like, an open family – certainly we have brought up a large family as freely as possible. In worldly terms the results can hardly be regarded as impressive, but one must hope that in other terms something valuable has been achieved.

Most of all, I think, there is encouragement in the way each of our children has set out to do their own thing, no matter how successfully or unsuccessfully – surely what life is all about. Some may never attain pinnacles, for others the chance remains. Demelza, one has an instinctive feeling, is forever on the brink in her musical career, of reaching the heights: friends who have seen her performing at the Venue or with Mike Oldfield or Stevie Winwood are astonishingly impressed at her abilities and surely such devotion to an art will find its ultimate reward – though whether this will help to bring the same fulfilment in personal life is another matter. For Genevieve, contrariwise, I like to think that there awaits some marvellous and as yet undreamed of fulfilment in a personal relationship, or a new way of life.

So it goes on, one's mind rambles round in circles, sitting indeed at a circular table surrounded by a circular family about whose beginnings and ends one becomes increasingly vague with the relentless passage of time. The one thing that our family have established unmistakably, is – *we shall not be overcome*! Or to put it a rather more salutary way, long after

Jess and I have passed into what other worlds await us some memory of us will be spreading eternally through the world around. It is, I think, a nice thought, even a kind of comfort, for ageing parents who must, every now and then, suppress a secret wistful sigh for all the future occasions they will never know.

Thinking on these lines, I suppose because I must be more egotistical than Jess who seldom seems bothered about such things, I often wonder what my children will think some time in the future, in more mature years, when they look back on such literary work as I have produced. It is difficult to make a comparison: my own parents were neither writers or artists, and so I had nothing to look back upon in that way. My father, on the other hand, though I was estranged from him, was quite a flamboyant figure in the world of flying and long after his death I have found myself secretly quite proud of his achievements, as I understand them better with my own maturity. Perhaps, I like to think, some time long hence, some of my children will start picking up odd books of mine – after all they will have about fifty to choose from whatever may happen now! – suddenly finding themselves caught up, interested, even who knows fascinated. Is this being conceited? I do not really think so: every artist is the best valuer of his own work. I know certain books to be good and worthy ones: *The Sea's in the Kitchen*, my first autobiography, *The Petrified Mariner*, my first total account of our long-range cruising in *Sanu*, *The Timeless Land*, a serious attempt to confine the relationship between Cornwall and the artists who have come to work there; among fiction, *A Company of Three*, a novelised treatment of a real happening, and *Barbican's End*, an attempt to pin down the Cornish myth in the form of fiction; plus of course half a dozen volumes of short stories which in my heart of hearts I would think to be the best of my writing.

Which of these or other books my children may later come to like I cannot possibly guess: what I do know, less happily, in the present day, is that by and large none of them are very interested at all. Perhaps this is only to be expected; growing up in a world where your father disappears into an office every day just like any other father going out to work, it is natural to think of the writing as just another job – and so, indeed, it is. Unfortunately writers tend to have vast egos, and I remain convinced that nobody in the family is really very interested in what I do or write (indeed whether I do or not). Perhaps it is unworthy of me. On the other hand I *am* rather encouraged into thinking on these lines, indeed sometimes speaking my mind in this fashion, by the endless stream of unsolicited testimonials which often come in from outside. The other day such a remarkable letter arrived from out of the blue (the Midlands in fact) that I am going to take the liberty of quoting it *in toto*, preserving the author's anonymity:

Dear Mr Val Baker:
    I hope you will forgive the intrusion of yet another fan letter. I have been prompted to write as a result of reading *A Family For All Seasons* in which you are more critical than usual of visitors. Before writing further, let me say that your criticisms make thoroughly good reading in themselves, and maybe such invasions can be extremely hurtful to one's privacy, but you do write as though such readers are eccentric which makes me wonder whether you appreciate fully the far reaching effect of your writing.
    Let me introduce myself briefly. I am just the wrong side of forty with a family and work as Production Control Manager at a major car factory. I also teach Business Studies, including industrial psychology. My spare time is taken up with Church activities, having studied to become an Anglican Lay Reader.
    I don't consider myself way out; I haven't much sympathy with drop-outs, I know nothing about Cornish writers (except perhaps Derek Tangye) or about boats or pottery. Your views on marriage and the meaning of life are not mine and yet I find that although I read about 20 books a year of which 17 are technical and theological and the rest fiction, even though reading time is precious, I invariably have a standing order placed for your latest book. I have

read all your autobiographical books except *The Sea's in the Kitchen* and *The Door is Always Open*. These two have been unobtainable locally although of course some of the events of the former are covered in a chapter of another of your books.

Year after year I anxiously await the next round of events. No doubt much is attributable to your literary style although I don't enjoy your short stories too much. More than anything else I think it is the candour with which you describe family events, even though so many are the kind of skeletons in the cupboard which the average person would want to keep there. Added to this is your refreshing interpretation of your thoughts and reasons for action.

I've already said that I frequently find it hard to agree with the attitudes and outlook you describe and yet I have undoubtedly learnt more tolerance of the unusual from reading your books and, I think, more confidence from being able to relate my own everyday problems and decisions to someone who has been honest enough to put their own experiences – good or bad – on paper. Most of us undoubtedly live in a world of subterfuge. We put on a show in front of neighbours, friends and workmates. We hide the anxieties; family, money, health problems, and tend to think we live in isolation, when in fact almost everyone has a cross to bear, a problem or anxiety to deal with or live with.

To return to my reason for writing; I am sure I am not alone, after regularly following your family's episodes, in feeling that you have all become very real folk, people of my own time, faced with the same world as I am faced with. I am surely not alone in feeling that I can share in the joys, uncertainty, worry, sadness, adventure and dreams that you describe, in much the same way that I would if a relative were writing on the same lines.

You expressed surprise last year at the many letters you receive from complete strangers. Can I suggest that when a writer chooses to bare his heart as you do that you cannot remain such a stranger, at least to them. Has it occurred to you that many of your readers know more (or feel they know more) about you, than about their husband/wives in as much as conversations have to be taken at face value. The thought process is not revealed.

It is no surprise that your last book but one prompted such a response. Having read through the various traumas experienced in your family over the years, usually ending reasonably satisfactorily, there you were, obviously run down and in a bad state of health, your family having spread their wings to various parts, your wife pursuing her studies away from home, your beloved boat deteriorating on a distant shore and the very definite impression of impending financial disaster. Who could fail to be moved by such a situation? Even though I knew it must be many months after the events I felt constrained to pray for strength and release from anxiety for you and your loved ones. Ridiculous, praying for a complete stranger? But you *are* a real person with real feelings and needs, and were, I believe, in special need. After all, I probably know more about your family than I know about the Royal Family for whom state prayers are said every day!

It was such a pleasure to read your next long awaited book. To learn of your wife's success and the partial resolving of some of your problems. (To have cleared them all up would rather detract the spice from your books!) Upon reflection I wonder if I am right in thinking that possibly the experiences related in your earlier books were written long after the actual events, resulting in most of the loose ends being tied up by the final chapter. In recent years the last chapter has left many unanswered questions and, like a film with a tragic ending, this is the one people remember and can relate to particularly as, unlike most stories, your story is happening now.

No, I don't think you can blame people for wanting to meet you. I am sure it is because they are really concerned, and because your writing represents a real part of their lives. Obviously it mustn't get so out of hand as to affect your family life more than momentarily, but if you are prepared to expose family details to the world at large it would be out of character for the man in the street if he were to show no concern or emotion.

Personally I would be hesitant about meeting you in case it shattered my illusions and spoil my current hope of many more years of anticipating your next book. On the other hand it would give me great pleasure to knock on your door, shake your hand and thank you for the fascinating world you have introduced me to through your writing. Certainly during one of my fairly regular trips to Devon or on the Continent I would go out of my way to have a look at *Sanu* in real life, or indeed one of the houses you have from time to time described. (But only from a discreet distance!)

It's an interesting twist, that just as you describe the many sorties from *Sanu* to visit historical and often mythical sites this rebounds in the sense that to the reader the writer becomes his representative – a living character of importance – and in turn the reader is left with a desire to see the objects described, to complete his appreciation with a visual experience of the house or boat he, through the joy of the written word, has grown to love.

May I conclude, not by apologising for my criticism; for I believe I know you well enough to sense that you would welcome practical criticism even though you may not agree with it. No, I would finish by congratulating you on mastering the art of making mundane, everyday topics and activities come alive. For perfecting a means by which your personal viewpoints, however odd or misplaced to your contemporaries, are in fact avidly read by them and perhaps even at times accepted.

I love your books. I respect and have a high regard for the characters you portray. May I wish you improved health and strength for many more years of adventure with your loved ones ...

Well, of course, I would not be human if I did not find such a letter most flattering. Perhaps, on the other hand, my own family's less than ecstatic attitude to my work makes a necessary and salutary counter-balance. Somewhere in between, I suspect, lies my proper place in life!

VI

Winter's Work is Never Done

When at last we saw in a New Year which was to mark the beginning of the 1980's and therefore I suppose should be regarded as a rather special occasion, my own personal luck seemed to run out. Over the years both Jess and I have experienced some pretty dismal New Year's Eves and even when the occasion has seemed not too bad there has often been some final twist to spoil the record. I am thinking as I write of a time about twenty years ago when we were in London and after spending a most convivial evening in Soho with two of our oldest friends, Ricky and Susan Richards, came out to find our car had been stolen!

In the very far distant past we used to attend a big arts dance at Hampstead, run on the lines of the famous Chelsea Arts Ball, and that I think is very much the way one should spend New Year's Eve – a time of near fantasy, of extravaganza, above all a party occasion. In more recent years whenever we have attended official New Year's Eve parties they usually seem to have lacked any real spontaneity. About two years previously for a change we thought we'd see in the New Year in a Cornish pub. We drove over to the Gurnard's head, near Zennor, where we knew a lot of artist friends would be gathered – but that, alas, proved a disappointment. Last year, however, we'd had a lucky break: as I described at length in *As The Stream Flows By*, a friend, Rosie Tempest, who had opened a wine bar in Penzance, decided to have a wine punch celebration where for £5 a head everyone was provided not only with as much punch and food as they could possibly want but with a first class cabaret act, 'The Barneys', plus honky tonk piano playing, folk singing, etc. On top of all this, it was a night of a great snowstorm and we only managed by great daring to find our way through six foot drifts along the Land's End road into Penzance so that even from the beginning there was a sense of achievement – to cut a long story short that had been a great and gay and totally successful New Year's Eve, a very rare event.

Now we were to fall back into the old pattern. At first we hoped to find some occasion like a repeat of last year's gathering: alas, Rosie was now eight months pregnant and hardly able to stage such an ambitious event. We poured over the pages of the *Cornishman* to see if there were any other public gatherings which might be worth attending (or for that matter could cope with a family of 11!) but the costs were totally prohibitive. We wondered whether to be content to hold our own gathering in the snug confines of the Mill House, but somehow on New Year's Eve one does have a feeling of wanting to be out and about, to share the occasion in a public way. In the end we decided on a compromise, to have a very pleasant slap-up meal at home first, and then to drive over to St Just to see in the New Year in one of the pubs there, the Star, where people were invited to attend wearing fancy dress on the theme 'Vicars and Tarts'. St Just is not a part of the world Jess and I often visit but in recent years it has become quite a centre for our young, partly I imagine because it is a cheaper area than St Ives or Penzance. At any rate the atmosphere in the pub was very congenial and quite a few people had gone in for very elaborate fancy dress costumes (even so I, with just a conventional vicar's white collar, appeared to be taken quite seriously by quite a few locals who, never having seen me before, I suppose took me for the real thing). Towards midnight Stephen started playing on the pub piano and there was a bit of a sing song. At least our whole family were together to see in the New Year ... but I have to confess it was with a whimper rather than a bang.

Mind you the fault was not entirely in the occasion. When Alan and Gill arrived from London they brought with them, apart from their lovely little daughter Amber and their

rather aloof cat, a virulent and infectious bout of flu. Poor
Amber went on suffering from it for several weeks, and Alan
too was quite knocked out by it initially. By New Year's Eve
he had recovered and was on the way to being his normal
ebullient self – little wonder since he had obviously passed the
whole thing over to me.

Sitting in the Star that momentous New Year, with a glass
of wine I could not even finish, the awful knowledge began to
dawn on me: *you're going down with flu*. There could be little
doubt about it: even before the bewitching midnight hour
struck my nose was streaming, my throat raw, my eyes
watering – yes, I had my first flu of the winter, brought down
of course from dusty London. I felt really miserable and
eventually must have communicated this to my companions.
Soon after seeing in the New Year Gill and Alan drove Jess
and me home before going off themselves to a party which had
been announced at the pub. At least they set off to look for it
but apparently spent nearly two hours driving round in circles
around Pendeen and Trewellard and Morva, before giving
up and returning home in disgust. It was that sort of evening:
at the party Demelza over-imbibed sufficiently to lose her cool
over some lost car keys and have a fit of hysterics so that for
days after no one would speak to her. Not a good New Year's
Eve!

A curious result of the flu with which I began the New Year
was an almost complete loss of my voice. This can be a strange
experience indeed. It has happened to me before, just for a day
or two, but on this occasion, possibly because I persisted in
trying to act as if nothing untoward had happened, what
began as a niggling temporary nuisance soon ran on into a
major irritation. I suppose it must always be a salutary
experience to lose, even temporarily, some regular and
important function. Each morning I would wake up after a
night of persistent coughing, hoping to hear my voice returned
to strength – only to find myself croaking out the same hoarse
monosyllables over the breakfast table. Unfortunately a lost
voice, like chilblains and several other unpleasant mishaps,
tends to be taken humorously by those around you, and it

seemed to me I received very minimum sympathy.

Jess's sole comment was: 'Fancy, I never before realised how much Denys talks – just listen, he can't stop trying even when he hasn't got a voice!'

This by the way was true, if unkind. Somehow, knowing I could not make myself understood, I found myself almost incessantly trying to babble on. Contrariwise it was most frustrating to have to repeat perfectly ordinary comments two or three times before they could be understood.

Worst of all were times on the telephone – which in my case are quite frequent. Owing to the ever-long holiday break normal business life was only just getting back to normal. At that time I had a particular anxiety over a book on the creative arts in Cornwall which I had been commissioned to write by one of the vast publishing complexes which now appear to dominate the publishing world. It was one of those books which my friend Peter Kimber always viewed with suspicion but, as in the case of a previous idea which he turned down, *The Sea Survivors,* I hoped to prove him wrong about this lack of enthusiasm. Actually, as ever with anything about Cornwall, I much enjoyed writing the book, trying to show what it was that drew so many creative workers down to my adopted home county. I had also gone to a lot of trouble, at the publisher's request, to assemble a huge selection of very good photographs of writers, painters, works of art, Cornish landscapes, sea views, local industries, above all mysterious carns and such edifices that typify Cornwall's truly mysterious qualities. I had spent a lot of time and trouble contacting dozens of photographers. It was all the more upsetting now to hear that following some interior upheaval within the particular publishing empire most of the people I had originally dealt with had vanished into limbo, and their replacements seemed to have quite different ideas about most things, including my book.

Fortunately the latter was too far gone as far as I was concerned; that is, I had written it and it was contracted and would be published. The photographs, it turned out were another affair altogether; suddenly a figure of up to a hundred was being whittled down to a mere handful or so. This was very embarrassing for me, as I felt I had let my photographer friends down. Hence all my angry phone calls to London – in my new croaking voice.

Talking to friends, likewise, suddenly presented a new problem. Quite without thinking on the first Monday in January I went into Penzance for my usual twice weekly meeting with my old friend Bill Picard – only to find that I had to sit and listen to him helplessly. At least I would have been *wiser* to have sat and listened! What happened, of course, was that doggedly I kept trying to talk, to give gossip for gossip, news item for news item ... by the time I returned home I had practically no voice left!

All this must sound comic, but at the time it became less and less so, especially when Jess would demand crossly that I should ring up so-and-so and see what had happened about this or that ... in my customary obliging way I would make the phone call, only to realise too late that I could hardly make myself understood. Funnily enough I found I received more sympathy on the phone than anywhere else – I can only suppose that such an instrument amplified one's suffering. The whole thing was given a grotesque ironic twist, when Frank Baker rang up to bemoan the fact that he and Kate had had a terrible Christmas and New Year, and that he had gone completely deaf in one ear and could only partly hear in the other. What an end for Frank and myself – the dumb and the deaf!

One of the reasons I needed my voice at this time was the continued vacillation on the part of our insurance company over the damage done during the storms at the beginning of December. The assessors had been out within a week and a figure had been agreed on for the damage: we had signed the requisite forms, and had been given to understand that the cheque would arrive within days, even before Christmas perhaps. On the strength of this assurance we had made arrangements for the rebuilding work to go ahead – only to find now, five weeks later, we still had not had a penny, whereas the builders simply had to be paid week by week. In desperation I rang the assessors and they swore black and blue that they had sent off their report and our agreement to the insurance company. Suspense, suspense – when I rang the insurance company they swore, equally emphatically, that the assessors had still not sent off their report. After about three or four double phone calls of this nature it became clear to me that there was the age-old example of one of the familiar British 'diseases'. At the time of writing, more than two months after the event, we were still waiting impatiently for settlement.

Curiously enough this turn of the year week also witnessed yet another disaster of the elements, this time one literally special to our corner of the woods. Apart from the two alarming gales our winter months had been comparatively mild so that we had almost forgotten about that perennial problem of ours – flooding. Now, over a single night, it all happened. Torrential rains of the previous afternoon and evening, instead of dying away as forecast, kept relentlessly on throughout the night ... When we woke up and looked out of the window our lawn had disappeared beneath the waters of the River Penberth, bursting their banks in all directions. As usual the water above the house was quite terrifying in its force, frothing and swirling madly as it tumbled down over rocks. At one stage the leat stream overflowed and cascaded around the back of the house but by and large it was a situation experienced regularly each winter and we knew there was not a great deal we could do except keep an eye on things and wait for the level to subside.

Demelza and Genevieve, however, had not been present on such previous occasions. Consequently they were more than a little disturbed when they woke up and found the caravan literally surrounded by water. I must say it made an extraordinary sight, the long green caravan at the end of the garden standing like an island amid the swirling torrents. The girls weren't in any real danger, of course, as the caravan was mounted on concrete blocks that raised it about two feet off ground level while the water, though frothing about sometimes up to a foot or so in depth, was constantly on the move downwards on its inevitable journey towards the sea. Mind you, as Demelza pointed out apprehensively, there was a garden wall beyond the caravan that did seem momentarily to hold back quite large quantities of water.

'Really, it isn't anything to worry about, Demelza,' I said soothingly. 'Your caravan won't be washed away, I assure you.'

This being a classic example of the occasion when a Virgo might blow her top, Demelza proceeded to do just that, and for the next half hour she had Stephen and Jess and me and Genevieve and anyone else unfortunate enough to be around running madly backwards and forwards, moving this and that. At one stage she ordered us to completely remove the bridge from across the stream, joining her part of the land to ours, and while this did enable the stream to flow more freely it also completely cut the girls off until the stream went down.

One way and another it was quite an exciting day and although the rain had stopped much earlier it was nearly dark before the level of water at last began to go down. When it did so, of course, there were many sorry sights, like the banana tree bedraggled and lifeless, and many new plants which Melza and Jess had planted either dead, dying or severely wounded.

Ah well, that's country life for you! One thing which the experience did prod us into was tackling the problem of our lane from the main road to the house. For some years past now we had all talked endlessly about improving the lane – an euphemism if ever there was one, for in recent months what had originally been gentle undulations had developed into pock-marked pits, some of them four or five inches deep. Our car springs jangled and protested every time we drove up and down, while most of our friends had long ago given up visiting us – or if they did so, were careful to leave their cars at the other end of the lane.

Things really had become impossible: Nevertheless I am afraid to the end I indulged in a shameful *laissez faire* attitude, mainly because somehow or other our little Vauxhall Viva seemed to survive all the bumps. This time though we had a catalyst present in the presence of our daughter Gill. I was reminded of a time two years ago when *Sanu* reached Rhodes in a sinking state, water flooding into the saloon ... we had been emptying out with buckets for hours until we were completely exhausted, yet when we appealed to local officials on the quay they just shrugged and wouldn't help. The rest of us were inclined to give up in despair but not tough little Gill. Off she marched to beard the harbourmaster in his office and forced him to take her to the Fire Brigade – a few minutes later a huge fire engine drew up opposite *Sanu* and within a very short time we were pumped dry.

It was rather like that now. While the rest of us went on saying, 'Yes, we really *must* do something about the lane,' Gill grimly pored over the Yellow Pages, ringing up one haulage firm after another. Mind you, I did keep inserting every now and then the relevant information that on a previous occasion soon after we first came, we had had a satisfactory load delivered by a local man, Mr McCary, and I felt sure he would be willing to repeat the service.

'Very well,' said Gill bad-temperedly, after her fourth refusal, 'What's his number? I'll ask him to bring a load tomorrow morning.'

Miraculously, at nine o'clock the next morning Mr McCary was at the other end of the lane with seven or eight tons of 'rab', a white powdery substance obtained from Geevor Mine at St Just, stuff which had the advantage over gravel that it packed down under weight and did not get pushed away by car wheels.

It was, of course, a pretty hectic morning. Owing to the narrowness of our lane and a previous unfortunate experience when he nearly lost his lorry in a ditch Mr McCary was unwilling to venture down the lane, so he dumped the rab across the end entrance. Meantime Stephen went and fetched his Morris Traveller, Alan, Rick and Jess and others took up spades and rakes, and we began a series of journeys in the Traveller dumping loads at various points and then spreading them out. In the end the load filled up about half the lane, so it was arranged that Mr McCary should bring a second load the following Monday morning. By then, alas, Gill and Alan and Rick and Jane had gone back to London, and as I had to go into Penzance Jess and Stephen were mainly responsible for the exhausting task of finishing the job. But at least it had been a job worth doing, for at the end of it suddenly we appeared to be driving down a road like any other road – well, almost!

Installing the caravan, setting up Alan's studio, building a garden shed, working on the wheel – what else were the busy bees buzzing about that winter? Well I must not forget a passing mention of Rick's pet project, a tree house he used to work on with Ben every time he came down. Somehow the tree house never seemed to progress very far, though this time it acquired a roof, but did provide a good deal of fun and amusement.

Before Jane and Rick returned to London, we had one final family get-together that proved especially enjoyable. Conscious of having enjoyed so much other hospitality during the week, Demelza and Genny insisted on our all coming over to their caravan for a farewell meal. Well – eleven people constitutes quite a crowd in a room, let alone in a caravan whose sitting area measures eight feet wide by about eighteen feet long. Yet, delightfully, from the moment we all crowded into the snug little place everything went off marvellously.

In planning the caravan Demelza had got Stephen to fit a Georgian window at one end, matching this with a curved seating area that could accommodate about eight people quite comfortably. Now, with us spread out there, and the other two or three grabbing stools, we formed a cosy group who were told to stay where we were while Genny and Demelza served up a most impressive meal of cheese pie and vegetables (followed by an exotic cream cake) on some of Genny's magically decorated plates. With the little wood stove burning brightly, candles flickering in the background, a glass of wine in every hand raised to toast the hosts, we proceeded to make the most of one of those rather unforgettable evenings that linger on in the memory for a very long time. All the minor family irritations seemed to have vanished and in their place there reigned a most pleasing and unusual harmony and peace!

Alas, life can be rather cruel. The day after this cheerful family gathering Demelza and Genevieve packed everything into their car and made the long drive back to London – arriving at Demelza's flat in Kensington to find that while they had been away burglars had paid a visit. And paid a visit with a vengeance: they had smashed down a steel door, broken a top window, literally broken their way into a flat which was packed with valuable antiques which had been collected over many years past.

It soon became obvious that the burglary was on a large scale and Demelza called in the police to inspect, though they seemed rather baffled. Since the flat is tucked away above a shop and its existence not easily recognised there was conjecture that someone who knew the girls, or at least mixed in their circles, must have been behind the crime. Either way it was a most disturbing experience – as Demelza said, it left you feeling rather as if you had been raped. What upset her particularly was that the thieves had not merely taken valuable *objets d'art* which at least were insured, but also her entire collection of personal tapes, which were truly irreplaceable.

So, having just popped back to London for a few days, Demelza and Genny found themselves immediately bogged down in long drawn-out negotiations with police and insurance officials, and their return had to be delayed for two or three weeks while they attempted to sort the mess out and find exactly what had been stolen. Meanwhile back at home I was burying myself, whenever illness allowed, into literary work. One pleasant surprise was the arrival of a page proof copy of *Women Writing: Three* which, as I wrote in my introduction 'confirms the establishment of this collection of short stories by leading women writers of today as an annual event'. Publication had now been taken over by Sidgwick and Jackson, an old established firm that specialised in rather literary books, and one improvement they had already agreed to was the use of a photograph of each author at the beginning of each story. Somehow I felt this made the collection a much

more personal affair, and indeed I found it endlessly
fascinating to thumb through the volume studying the varying
portraits of those formidable writers from older and worldly-
wise faces like those of Mary Renault and the late Jean Rhys,
to pretty, younger ones like Angela Huth and Julie Welch.
Almost every photograph was a revealing one: Margaret
Drabble, Lynne Reid Banks, Penelope Gilliatt, etc., – they all
looked women of imagination and perspicacity who would be
most interesting to meet. As an editor – partly I suppose
because I live in rather a remote part of the country – I seldom
meet my authors. On the other hand we frequently indulge in
the most entertaining correspondences, and only recently
with some relief had I managed to round off a most vigorous
exchange of irate letters between Mary Renault and myself.
All's well that ends well, but in between ...! Nearly every
author I chose to deal with as an editor (men and women for
that matter) I have found not merely courteous and friendly,
but usually amusing and entertaining as well. Perhaps, who
knows, these relationships by proxy are really the best. But
then as Jess says this is my weakness, I do tend to shy away
from the personal contact.

Perhaps the sweetest of all the photographs in *Women
Writing: Three*, and I am sure the other contributors won't
mind my saying so, was an Edwardian one of a beautiful
young girl with her head carefully done up in a bun at the
back. This was the Welsh authoress, Kate Roberts,
photographed many decades ago, as a demure young lady –
now, in her *eighties* she is very much the doyenne among Welsh
writers. To this day she writes her stories in the Welsh
language, and in her own country has a stature that purely
English writers might well envy. But then of course (speaking
as a Welshman exiled) the Welsh must be the most literary
race in the whole British Isles. I mean: Dylan Thomas,
Vernon Watkins, Kate Roberts, Richard Hughes, Glyn Jones,
Gwyn Jones, Richard Llewellyn, Caradoc Evans, Margiad
Evans, R.S. Thomas – need I go on? Well, perhaps I ought to,
as over my shoulder I hear someone shouting in broad Irish a
few names like James Joyce, Frank O'Connor, Liam

O'Flaherty, Sean O'Faolian, Brendan Behan, etc. Yes, yes, maybe it's a moot point. All one can say really is that the British are a lucky people indeed to foster such talents.

Would that Cornwall could be included among such lists! I fear, as I must have mentioned in earlier books, that local literary talent is sparse on the ground. Indeed most of the 'Cornish' authors who have made any mark have been 'foreigners' like myself who have been happy enough to plant roots here, but can never pretend to be natives. Among true natives there are a few notable figures – one of them, the poet D.M. Thomas, I am pleased to see has been gaining due recognition recently. Perhaps, indeed, just to show that Cornwall does have its voices I may end this chapter by quoting a few lines from one of his many visually exciting poems which I printed in the *Cornish Review:* 'A Sea Child of Perranporth.'

> Karenza is my name. If you betray me,
> expect no pity when the midnight moon steps forth
> and you behold me, or my enantiomorph,
> waiting for you and singing on the shore.
> My eyes, whites black as chert, will lure
> as a ship is tide-drawn to an old wharf
>
> at the tin-stream's outlet. From Bude to Geevor,
> whatever land-child you are lying with,
> you will hear a sea-child call you. Faithless wrecker,
> you will stumble down the seaward-sloping path,
> and there, by tide and rock cut off,
> trample through the red sea-running mirror,
> to find all changed ...

VII

Searching for a New Life

Although the 1970's down in Cornwall did not at first seem greatly different from the preceding decade it is possible in restrospect to appreciate that life was definitely taking a slant in the direction of what might be called 'Back to nature'. This of course has been happening all over the world, and a good thing too. Instinctively people are beginning to draw back from blindly following paths of technology that can only lead to disaster not merely for the few but indeed for the whole world. God knows our political leaders have made enough mess of things – perhaps now the time has come for much more personal involvement in trying to direct life into a healthier direction. The main fear is that it is too late, and that the prospect of a mad world full of hideous nuclear strike weapons lined up in rows pointing east and west, though ostensibly too terrible to contemplate, is unfortunately the reality which faces us – the only possible end result an ultimate holocaust.

At least in Cornwall we are able to preserve a certain illusion of escape. Not for us, as in unfortunate East Anglia, the prospect of harbouring a couple of hundred of travelling warheads! Mind you, we do have our environmental problems. Strong local rumours have it that oil prospecting in what is prettily termed 'the Celtic Sea' is either in progress or about to start. Similarly, schemes are forever being propounded for one kind of development or another guaranteed to further erode the charm and uniqueness of Cornwall and its mysterious world.

Nevertheless there has recently been this very pronounced

movement back to the more natural life. This was epitomised for me in the appearance of several local publications, like the lively little *Alternative Cornwall* in which were brought together details of all sorts of progressive movements, lectures, dramas, concerts, etc. As a one time editor of the other local magazine *Cornish Review* I was pleased to notice a great improvement in several contemporaries, such as the pictorial *Cornish Life* in which it seemed to me the real life of the county was at last being explored in more depth, and the bi-monthly *The Cornish Chough*.

Somehow this latter title suggested something either parochial or at least nationalistic, but in fact I was pleasantly surprised to find the contents unusually enlightened, with articles on compost growing of vegetables, the need for wholesome bread, how to make the best use of the land generally, as well as in-depth studies of psychology, modern medicine and similar subjects that are of real importance to the individual. It has always seemed to me that it is in remote areas like Cornwall that what are popularly known as alternative modes of life may best be put into practice. Of course there is always the risk that such things are taken up as 'fashions', and I am sure this does happen here and there, but one gets the feeling that such organisations as the Ecological Party of Britain, with its headquarters at Wadebridge, or various community groups dotted over other parts of Cornwall, are endeavouring to lay the seeds of worthwhile new life.

Ever since we set up life together, Jess and I have been drawn to the whole idea of community movements and co-operative ventures. This phase reached its peak a couple of decades back when we were living in St Ives – our children still in their early teens or even younger – and both Jess and I had become very disillusioned with the trend of world events. We had just been through the experience of the Cuban crisis, but even before that we had both been active supporters of the Campaign for Nuclear Disarmament, taking part in several inspiring gatherings in Trafalgar Square and so on. Even though such experiences had been encouraging, reviving one's faith in the essential goodness and common sense of ordinary people, as parents of a large young family we couldn't help being worried about future prospects.

At that time we had developed a close friendship with Ken and Jane Moss and their friend Mud. Ken was later to help me launch the *Cornish Review*, and between us, at some stage, we began to think about the idea of setting up a pacifist community. Not, obviously in England, which appeared likely to be involved in some dreadful holocaust – but on the other side of the world, in New Zealand. I forget now quite what made us settle on New Zealand. We had probably heard that it was a rich and fertile land, with a climate neither tropical nor sub-tropical but temperate and variable, and so obviously a place offering great scope.

In particular we were drawn to the idea of trying to make a new start on an island, encouraged no doubt by the knowledge there were literally dozens of them scattered around the long and tortuous coastline of New Zealand. By now we had decided that the north of New Zealand might suit us better than the south, somewhere in the region of Auckland, and so I began bombarding the local estate agents, setting out our rather unusual requirements. Back came several letters, among them one which we realized at once was really important. It was headed rather magnificently: Dalgety and New Zealand Loan Ltd., with an address in Auckland. telling us that they had for offer a block of land comprising 12,000 acres situated on the Great Barrier Island which is 60 miles from the port of Auckland and approximately 25 miles due east from the mainland. The climate is almost sub-tropical. The block comprised about 4,000 acres of cleared land, i.e. cleared of bush, and 8,000 acres of native bush; the island was a fairly large one with a resident population of approximately 350 people. The asking price was £10,000.

We looked at one another excitedly. Great Barrier Island – it was a romantic enough name. Was this to be the answer to our problems? We wrote off eagerly for more details, tabulating a formidable list of questions, some exotic about any wild animals we might encounter and so on, some more mundane about building restrictions and rates. All of them were answered painstakingly.

With their letter Dalgety sent along a pen and ink map of Great Barrier, showing in red ink the extent of what already, secretly, we thought of as 'our property'. Studying the map was like taking part in some ancient treasure island game: it was marked here and there with fascinating tit-bits 'copper mine' (in the north, 'native bush', 'hot springs', 'reclaimable swamp', 'amphibious plane landing point', and so on. There were also one or two more mundane markings – 'District Nurse' and 'store' – to remind us that this particular island might be a handy compromise between the harsh primitive-starting-life-afresh sort of place and the more general amenities of life. We thought, looking around at our rather unprimitive selves, this might be just as well.

Things were beginning to move. Personally, I found that the project seemed to have taken possession of my whole life. I no longer had any time to write stories, or hardly so – I was too busy embarking on massive correspondences, not only with Dalgety, but with various other sources we began to approach, trying to get an all-round picture of Great Barrier Island. In quick succession I wrote to the Department of Agriculture, Wellington, the editor of the *New Zealand Farmer*, the Clerk of the Great Barrier Island Council, the Secretary of the Great Barrier Development Association, the founders of an existing Community, Riverside, in New Zealand – and to a New Zealand poet (of Cornish descent) I remembered meeting when he visited Cornwall, Allen Curnow.

From the Department of Agriculture we had a long, very factual letter about the numbers of sheep etc, but the editor of the *New Zealand Farmer* was rather more down to earth and after giving a lot of practical information emphasized that he could not argue too strongly that one of us should come out as an advance guard first to determine what problems we would be confronted with 'and what handicaps you will come up against on an area like the Great Barrier which beautiful as it is, and probably idyllic for an attempt at community living, is restricted in economic development to a very few pastoral products'.

From Frank O'Brien, secretary of the Development Association we had an amusing yet somehow encouraging account of his own efforts to unify the opinions and actions of the rugged individualists who live on Great Barrier: he also put us in the picture about our particular property, which had originally been offered at £22,000, and was no doubt open to an offer even lower than the present reduced figure of £10,000, as the owners were obviously very anxious to sell. Finally my friend Allen Curnow wrote a cheery note to confirm his willingness to help anyway, and mentioning that Great Barrier was very beautiful. 'What an Aucklander calls a "nice beach" is something both lovelier and lonelier than Waikiki (which I've seen) or the Riviera (which I haven't)'.

But perhaps the communication that in many ways gave us most heart was a note from Arch Barrington of the Riverside Community, near Motueka, enclosing a formidable illustrated sixteen-page brochure about the Community's activities. In a comparatively short time, since the war, the members had developed the community into a property of 550 acres, and were now engaged on a variety of work – bee-keeping, fruit farming, sheep rearing, dairying, pigs, poultry, timber milling, engineering. Once an individual or a family had been admitted into full membership they were guaranteed, 'free, good and adequate independent accommodation, all farm produce, a monetary allowance graduated according to size of family to provide a standard of living equal to a good average working-class family in present day society, the payment of all taxes, medical, dental, optical expenses; electric light and power; and transport'. At the back of the booklet there was an aerial photograph of the community, showing a handsomely laid out establishment with hostels, a packing shed, workshops, tennis court, etc – even a roadside stall for the direct sale of produce. In short the Riverside, which was by the way primarily a Christian community, was a highly organized and successful venture. As we studied the account of their work, although we realized that in many ways we would disagree philosophically, we felt a great admiration for the progress that had been achieved.

Could we do the same? Obviously there was a great deal of

preparation work to be done before we could set about gathering in other members of the community. First, we agreed, we should assemble together the basis of a practical plan, so that we had something to offer. At least it seemed that we had fixed upon a suitable country – New Zealand. Now, too, it appeared that by a stroke of luck we had found what might well be an ideal site. But before going any further, naturally, we were anxious to find out more still about Great Barrier. I wrote to a photographic agency in Auckland, asking them to supply any photographs they might have of the island. A little while later a large square packet arrived, and we all gathered together to witness this first visual encounter with 'our island'.

There were three large aerial photographs. I unwrapped them one by one, and handed them round, in silence.

'Oh,' said Jess.

'Mmmh,' said Ken.

'Aaaah,' said Mud.

'Ah, well,' said Jane, always the most optimistic of us. 'It's only from the air, isn't it?'

We clung somewhat dubiously to this crumb of comfort: for the truth was never had we seen three such derelict and barren landscapes. One showed what seemed an impenetrable range of grim, craggy mountains: another showed a huge lonely pock-marked valley; only the third, with a distant view of the sea and long white rollers pounding on a wide sandy beach, looked at all inviting. It was true, we kept telling ourselves that an aerial photograph might not do justice to the actual scenery. What we really needed were some ground-level photographs. Better still a movie film – we looked longingly at our own cine camera. Ah, if only we could take a film of Great Barrier, or get one taken.

We supposed, at considerable expense, it might be possible to organize this, paying a photographer from Auckland to go over. However, just about this time by a stroke of luck our daughter Gill, given a lift by a young merchant seaman, John Brooks, discovered that he was about to join his ship for a voyage to – New Zealand. Furthermore, he was mad about the area, had even been past Great Barrier, thought highly of our efforts, and would be only too glad to pay a visit when he got out there. It would be about six weeks before he got out to New Zealand, but then his boat would be docking at Auckland for a while, and he hoped to persuade the captain to lend him one of the boat's whaling boats so that he could get across to Great Barrier. He proposed to borrow a cine camera and spend several days on the island, and would then air mail the film back to us.

Meantime the letters kept winging backwards and forwards across the world: from the estate agents, from the Department of Agriculture, from the Customs agents, from all kinds of people, both personal and official. Among them we had a friendly letter from an Auckland accountant, Mr C.A. Howell, who had been told by the Riverside Community of our venture and offered to help on the business side. Already he had taken the trouble to approach some local makers of prefabricated building and now sent us some catalogues to study. He promised also to go into the whole question of farm machinery etc.

In the same post an absorbing letter from an enterprising spirit, one Lloyd Morris, who with his wife was apparently touring the whole of New Zealand on a motor-cycle, visiting various community centres. He had already been to Riverside and Beeville and had encountered several other prospective groups. While touring he had also heard of two possible new sites – the most interesting being Te Paki station, 43,000 acres, consisting of Cape Reinva and surrounding property at the North Tip of North Island, an area with miles of beaches on the east and west coasts, views from the high hills out over the ocean, pine woods and numerous creeks that run down to the ocean. Lloyd Morris was anxious to know more of our plans, and informed us, on the basis of his investigations, that he had found that most people regarded the all-in-common basis as the great drawback of community life, both because of the loss involved if they wished to leave and the restriction of individual initiative while a member. 'It is often possible only to try experiments or innovations at one's own expense and this is only possible where there is an individual income and time can be bought by reducing living costs and saving.'

Lloyd Morris's letter was one of several we had from others who were interested in community life. There was a most interesting letter from Mrs Betty Block, of Kerikeri, north of Auckland about the experiences of her and her husband in running a small community:

> Our property is of 70 acres with a small citrus orchard, some grassland, plantations, etc., situated on a long and lovely coastline – my husband has started a pottery which is very successful and I am making and selling ceramic jewellery and hand-tinted fabrics and recently began spinning and weaving.

We also made contact with E.D. Gregory, of Henderson, near Auckland, another pacifist who had made a study of community life and was most anxious to help us in any way possible. He was a member of the New Zealand Peace Council and the New Zealand Labour Party, and appeared most knowledgeable, even about Great Barrier, of which, though, he took a guarded view – 'Perhaps' he wrote:

> you have a sentimental view because of the early Cornishmen who settled there to work the copper mines. I have met some of them but few remain on Barrier today ... It is wilder than Dartmoor. The type of land you propose to take over has all the disadvantages of those areas and little advantages, save isolation. Personally I would favour north of Auckland, where there are outcrops of clay suitable for pottery making. A good location would be near the sea. I know of several locations and will be glad to investigate.

'I like the sound of Mr Gregory,' said Jess firmly. 'He's a realist, we ought to ask his advice.'

A little uneasily, for I had surmised indeed that Mr Gregory was a very honest realist, I wrote and asked. Back came another breezy letter in which our new friend explained just why he had doubts about Great Barrier. We had by now cheerfully told him of John Brooks's impending visit.

> I wonder whether or not your photographing friend knows Great Barrier? He will require a horse, or be willing to do much walking in rough country where he will need to camp out perhaps two or three nights. It will be easy to get yards of film in the settled areas but your area is a wilderness.
>
> As you say, the Barrier settlers are 'rugged individualists' and that denotes a die-hard Tory attitude which is present among all the farmers throughout New Zealand. This raises a question; will these Barrier people be well-disposed to you when they know your philosophy? My experience has been that those people who have lived in isolation long are the most intolerant.
>
> Don't forget weeds – do not think of these weeds in terms of English garden and field weeds. I have seen thistles 8 feet high, gorse often reaches 8 to 9 feet in unattended areas, and blackberries will form masses of growth that one cannot ride through. During summer these and other weeds would create serious fire hazards – the area you intend to settle on would need protecting by means of fire brakes, a tedious job when you have other work to do. In such an area there will be ample cover for rabbits and possum which can be plagues. Finally I must comment – that if you desire isolation and are prepared to be a self-contained community there is some feasibility in the scheme; but the effort will be greater than it need be.

We digested this letter carefully, trying to avoid horrific visions of an innocent young merchant seaman disappearing among a mass of eight feet high thistles and gorse bushes. We could hardly avoid recognizing the wisdom behind Mr Gregory's remarks, and perhaps just for a moment our fixation on Great Barrier Island began to waver. But then we pulled ourselves together – where was our pioneering spirit? The time had come, we felt, to start organizing our community membership. We wrote a letter to *Peace News*, and at the same time inserted advertisements in one or two local newspapers.

In the long run, as we imagined, the *Peace News* letter was to bring us the most interesting results, but in the meantime we found that our local appeal – for anyone interested in forming a co-operative community overseas – produced several immediate inquiries. We invited everyone interested to the first of a series of meetings in our front room looking over the glorious Porthmeor Beach, quite a suitable setting for planning such an exciting adventure. We had felt it only fair to invite everyone who took the trouble to inquire, but looking round we felt some unease; it was obvious that several had just come out of idle curiosity, while one or two others manifestly were not even really in sympathy with our ideals.

On the other hand this meeting resulted in our teaming up with at least two very keen and enterprising supporters, Douglas Rowe, and his wife Sheila, so the occasion was well worth while. Douglas, an agricultural diesel engineer, supplied just that touch of practical mechanical knowledge which we were only too conscious of lacking, and this, added to his abounding energy and enthusiasm, immediately gave us great encouragement.

Several others present seemed likely to be prospective members but as we talked together we began to discover the kind of problems which must inevitably bedevil such enterprises. One person, for instance, would like to come, but his wife wouldn't – another couldn't make up his mind whether or not to divorce his wife and come alone, and so on. With greater experience we would have been able to judge correctly that in such circumstances, inevitably the people concerned would never come – but at that time we had to find out these things by lengthy and cumbersome talks and meetings.

One half-member, as I might justly call him, mystified us for a long time by writing the most fascinating and enthusiastic letters, full of sound practical common sense about the market gardening side of our venture, well laced with impressive philosophic overtones – yet whenever he appeared he hardly spoke a word and gave no indication of really intending to come.

After one or two of these, on the whole, abortive local meetings we decided to concentrate on the long list of inquirers in response to my letter in *Peace News*. We had in the meantime produced a circular letter outlining our general aims, and our first step was always to send this together with a carefully designed questionnaire with cunning demands for details which we hoped would reveal their subconscious reasons for wanting to go as well as the practical use they could be.

We had devoted a great many evenings to working out the questions, learning some of our lessons from various other questionnaires which had been sent to us from time to time (though not going to the extremes of one organization which asked: Have you been psychoanalysed? Do you smoke? Do you drink? How much? How often? etc). It was surprising how often the use of the questionnaire helped to save a waste of both our own time and that of the inquirers, who by the very nature of their answers immediately established their unsuitability for joining such a community. Typical of these was the man who insisted, oddly, that there should be no Russian or South American members of the community: another was an arch-racialist, writing pages about the inferiority of the black people – why he ever applied in the first place goodness only knows. Then again there were some who, in their answers to question 15, or perhaps 20, showed what we considered a very reactionary attitude. However, I don't want to make it sound as if we were too hidebound in our approach: very few were originally rejected, and in most cases we arranged a meeting and discussion even with the doubtful ones. And the boot could well be on the other foot as transpired on several occasions – we didn't measure up to their requirements!

Now began a long and sometimes complicated series of meetings usually held at the weekends as most of the corresponders lived as far away as Birmingham or Norfolk or even Yorkshire. The fact that nevertheless, they were willing to make such a long journey made it obviously incumbent upon us to provide hospitality, so we took it in turn with the Mosses in putting up these unknown visitors. Just because they were unknown, of course, we couldn't help very often being a little nervous about the prospects, especially after one initial weekend where we got involved with a fanatical religious couple who used the name of Jesus Christ in every other sentence. Still, as against that we made several very useful contacts: notably with Hugh and Doreen Court, of Brighton, and the Gammons, of Harpenden, both young couples with young children, and eager to make a fresh start. The Courts drove down in their Dormobile and spent a lively weekend here, during which we had over one or two other prospective local members. We soon found ourselves expanding our plans, as Hugh was an architect, and immediately suggested planning the layout for a communal settlement. Dick Gammons was a librarian at Harpenden, but anxious to do something more creative, and he and his young wife offered to take on some of our organizing work, which by this time had become quite a full time occupation.

At Mud's suggestion we had decided to form ourselves into a kind of 'administration'. Each of us took on the responsibility for a specific feature of getting our community organized. Mud was to handle the transport problems, building was temporarily my concern (later passed on gladly to Hugh Court), Ken Moss looked after the financial aspect, Douglas Rowe took on the engineering side, Jane Moss the catering, while it was agreed that a pacifist farmer who had approach us, Alec Lea, might prepare the dairy farming plans.

It was surprising what a fantastic amount of planning was involved. In the sphere of building alone, for instance, I had to prepare a plan for setting up temporary accommodation immediately for up to sixty people and their children. This involved getting all kinds of technical magazines and writing to dozens of firms to get quotations and then working out elaborate costings.

In other spheres, Douglas Rowe was collecting masses of

information about tractors and other equipment ... Mud was trying to obtain the cheapest possible single fares to New Zealand, and also investigating the possibility of chartering a small cargo boat to take the lot of us ... and on the financial side, perhaps the worst problem of all, Ken Moss was trying to work out some estimates of what we would need totally. Almost every time we met, alas, this figure seemed to rise. Originally we had hoped that £20,000 might be enough, but gradually the estimate got nearer to £30,000 – while Ken himself thought even £50,000 might be a safe figure to aim at. Astronomical as this seemed, when between us in ready cash we could muster no more than a few hundred pounds we knew they were not beyond the bounds of possibility. Most of us owned houses, and it would simply be a question of selling up our homes to raise the final money. Nothing was impossible.

Around this time the national press began to take an interest in our scheme. We had never sought publicity of this kind, partly because we had a shrewd idea of the way many of the more sensational newspapers would present the matter. It is extraordinary, and I write as an ex-newspaper man, how perversely some national newspapers will slant a perfectly straightforward news story. I remembered noting how even *The Guardian* headed a story about a previous community group with the loaded headline '*Escapists Seek Dream Island*', which immediately caused a kind of antagonism in the reader's mind. Now, similarly, the *Daily Express* came out with a lurid headline: 'Ban-Bomb Men Plan to Buy Island: No More Sit-Downs. Ignoring the irrelevance of the sub-title, our group consisted of women as well as men, we were not necessarily all ban-the-bomb adherents, and anyway we were only proposing to buy a site on an island, not an island. Almost the first statement in the story, 'They all live in Cornwall' was again untrue, and the whole presentation seemed designed, whether consciously or unconsciously it would be difficult to say, to titivate the bored public's appetite.

Unfortunately from our point of view these and similar stories were picked up by overseas correspondents of the New

Zealand newspapers and sent back to be reprinted in papers like the *Auckland Herald*, thus giving a garbled version of our plans for people over there. Soon after this I had a letter from Frank O'Brien of the Great Barrier Development Association telling me, 'Wild rumours are circulating Great Barrier concerning your group – you would be surprised and amused at what you are supposed to be going to do!'

From our point of view publication of such misleading versions of our plans were no help, even though most of the people interested in such a venture were not likely to be influenced. A smear is always a smear, and leaves a nasty flavour. Still we were too busy on our plans to really worry. Almost every weekend was now devoted to meetings. One one occasion a party of thirteen, all members of one large family group, came down to explore possibilities of joining in with us. Fortunately they had rented a bungalow on Hayle Towans, so we were able to spread out on the dunes overlooking St Ives Bay while we talked. We found these gatherings often stimulating, but also sometimes rather disturbing. It was surprising what delicate differences of outlook and opinion, could exist, under the surface, between people nominally of the same general outlook. Sex, money, religion, pacifism – these seemed to be the four main bugbears. In particular, perhaps it came into focus in community planning, we were surprised how many of the men still clung to the old-fashioned ideas of a woman's place being in the kitchen. They seemed unable to comprehend the change in attitudes (reflected rather sweetly I feel among the teenagers, today, where there is a very real sense of sex equality).

But to tell the truth the philosophical problems seldom got much chance at this stage beside the enormous weight of the sheerly practical considerations. Just getting to New Zealand in the first place, when you went into the problem, became something of a nightmare. There were really very few boats, berths were booked up for as much as a year ahead, all the cheaper fares were gone, we could find nothing less than about £180 single per person – multiply that by about forty to fifty and even that figure alone became astronomical. Then when we got to Great Barrier we would have to set about erecting the portable buildings which, we hoped, we would have been able to arrange to have delivered there beforehand. We were in touch with two or three of the several large firms in Auckland which specialized in this work, but here again prices were hardly low. Hugh Court, the architect member, had meantime worked out some exciting plans for a circular settlement: in this sphere at least we felt surges of optimism. There could be no doubt that there would be something wonderful about a planned community with a real moral basis, as distinct from the corrupt society all around us; where each would contribute according to his capacity, and there would be a real sharing of the fruits of our labours.

A matter to which we had devoted a lot of thought, naturally, was the question of income. Many people who sneered at our project fixed on this as the stumbling block, imagining that we would be entirely dependent on what we could scrape from selling vegetables and fruit. But in fact we had heard too much about other communities' difficulties on these lines, and we were determined to evolve a method of deriving our income from *several* sources. This was not as difficult as it might seem. To begin with, I, as a writer, could still earn an income from writing, even if no doubt a reduced one. We planned to make pottery over there, too, and we had learned that pottery was much in demand. Another member planned to do weaving, and no doubt there would be one or two other crafts to bring in money. The agricultural side would, as well, bring in a certain income. Then there were possibilities for exploring new avenues, i.e. furniture making from our own timber. Finally, under the system in New Zealand, there was a family allowance of 75p a week per child, to which we would be fully entitled as we would be paying normal income tax and rates, etc. – and since we envisaged a group that included probably thirty children or so, this would in itself provide more than £1,000 a year.

So it appeared that the difficulties of our community, once it was set up, would not be financial ones. Once on Great Barrier, we firmly believed, we had a fair chance of success.

And so weekend after weekend, sometimes night after night, we pored over our plans feeling, I suppose, a little like old-time Pilgrim Fathers. Meanwhile, as a vital fuel to our planning the letters and dossiers kept passing to and fro, mainly from the estate agents. Dalgety's were now pressing for one of us to go out and see for ourselves: at the same time, being estate agents and anxious to achieve some sort of sale, they were constantly, if our attention seemed likely to flag, sending us details of fresh properties – notably the sixteen lovely Cavalli Islands, of which we saw a colour photograph (Price £25,000!). Our friend Mr Gregory, too, kept up a bombardment of letters, each one containing details of some more exotic and extraordinary property. If only we had had the ready cash, I believe we might have ended up owning several parts of New Zealand!

Money – that was the stumbling block, or so we told ourselves. On paper we could raise quite a bit between us: if we included everyone who had put down the sum they would contribute, we certainly had the price of our site, if not entirely the cost of fares out. But of course we knew we needed more. And even to raise what was offered would involve a drastic and immediate sell up of houses. Some of us might be able to make a quick sale, but others might hang fire – it was a kind of vicious circle. But this was the hub of it all, we felt sure.

And then there arrived in our midst one Mac Smith. To us at first it was just one of dozens of names, except that we did notice that the address was a far away one, up in Cumberland. However, even in his letters Mac communicated something of his alarming energy. Unlike most other approaches, his was a confident, positive one. Had we done this? Had we thought of that? Had we fixed a date of departure?

'Well, he sounds quite a live wire,' said Jane Moss tentatively.

'I don't like the sound of him,' said Mud.

Jess and Ken and I reserved judgment. We were impressed by the fact that in his next letter Mac proposed dashing down for one night (from Cumberland!) just to have a talk with us.

'He must be very keen ...'

In the meantime Mac had filled up the questionnaire and, if I remember right, hoped to be able to contribute quite a large sum, around £5,000. Our spirits began to rise. We wrote off applauding his initiative, and it was arranged that Ken Moss would pick him up at Penzance Station and Jess and I would drive over to Sennen for an evening meal.

For some reason I have always retained a vivid picture of the moment of our arrival that evening. Supper was already laid out, and around the table the others were seated, but somehow there was not quite the usual carefree atmosphere. We were not even met by the same friendly smiles and cheerful welcomes – no, the feeling in the air, if I can describe it with precision was one of – well, I think 'early exhaustion' might do.

And there, in the place of honour, sat the cause of this – our new member, Mac, a tall slightly balding man who exuded tremendous energy and seemed somehow very physical (I think, indeed, he wore a bright shirt and hiker's shorts). Here was no blushing lily, no quiet back-bencher – here indeed was a full-blown community organizer. Indeed Mac immediately began to tell us at some length how not long ago he himself had planned a community – advertising, rushing up and down the country, interviewing people – only to throw the whole thing up in disgust at people's dithering.

'That's what attracted me to you lot. You sounded direct, to the point. It's the only way.'

As the meal progressed and we became more used to Mac's sometimes aggressive manner, things warmed up. Here was no theoretical planner but a man who had worked a sheep farm, built his own house, laid his own drive, organized umpteen affairs – now and then tossing off a story for the radio almost as a spare-time occupation! We could not help being impressed even though the uneasiness persisted. Mac was obviously something of a human dynamo: we could imagine him bull-dozing his way through all problems. But how would other people react? Would his contribution to community life be exactly harmonious?

It was impossible to make up our minds in the course of a

single evening. Obviously Mac felt the same way, too, for the next day when we rang up Jane told us, in a rather strained voice, 'He's still here!' In point of fact Mac stayed several days, during which time his dynamism was temporarily applied to the situation around him. He had Ken and Mud at work on redecorating their front room under his directions and made a few peremptory suggestions for improving the domestic arrangements of the house, undeterred by the fact that at one stage the distraught Jane burst into tears!

By now Mud felt entirely confirmed in his first fears and even wrote a brief memo putting his views for Mac's consideration. It was pretty obvious, too, that the prospect of spending the rest of her life on a remote island with Mac did not appeal to Jane either. On the other hand Ken, a very fair-minded man, felt quite strongly that we probably needed someone like this, who would constantly spur us on and take practical initiatives. Jess and I were undecided, and spent another evening listening to Mac. This time we had Douglas Rowe also. We could see, on the strength of a first meeting, that Mac's practical attitudes appealed to him.

'Now let's stop beating about the bush,' said Mac, after the meal that evening. 'We want to go out to New Zealand, don't we? Right, then – let's go!'

'But ... the fares ... waiting list ... what about when we get there ... getting organized ...?'

'Pouff! Just make up your minds. Why, when I wanted to take the wife abroad some years back they told us there wasn't a hope of a berth on the ship for months ahead. So what did I do? I said, come on, we'll go down to the docks, and just wait. We'll get a berth ... And we did, too!'

Fixing his attention on Douglas, whom he obviously recognized as the only really practical one among us, Mac said brusquely:

'What about it, then? Are you ready? We'll catch a train up tomorrow, and get down to London docks. Don't worry, we'll get a berth. Never mind what they say about waiting lists.'

At that moment, nervously, we recognized the profound truth of this revolutionary suggestion.

Mac swept on, rather magnificently.

'It's all quite simple. We get out there *somehow*. Leave the women and children in Auckland, advance party get across – then *work*.' He almost glared at us accusingly. 'Moment we set foot on the land, it'll be just a case of hard slogging. No good thinking we can have any slacking either. What's more, it'll be like that for a long time – maybe for years. Just think of what's got to be done. Earth levelling, swamp draining, building work ...'

Why, even Mac's head was a little damp with sweat at the thought of it all – as for the rest of us, I think we felt limp already!

That evening under the stimulus of Mac's provocations, we really got down to some fundamentals. Many of his suggestions we disagreed with, as he did with many of ours – but I think we were forced to learn something from him despite his hectoring approach.

'He's right, you know,' said Mud, a day or two later when Mac had departed as abruptly as he arrived, bound on still more enormous journeys across half England. 'It's the only way. Get up and go – *tomorrow*.'

If I remember rightly there was even a period longer where we seriously went into the possibility of hiring several ex-Army lorries and driving our expedition across half the world, via an intriguing route that took in France, Italy, Yugoslavia, Greece, Turkey, Persia and so on, right through India and down to Singapore ... Yet in our hearts, I think perhaps we knew from the time of Mac's visit that we had come to the brink, and for one reason or another, depending on our own problems, we were unable to take the decisive step over the top. Our future plans, we suddenly realized, were too confined by 'ifs'. *If* we sold our house, *if* the Mosses sold theirs, *if* so and so gave up his job, *if* another couple really made up their minds, *if* the farmer renounced his farm – and so on. Indeed, *if* our community might well have become a fact. Between us, on paper, we had the money, and many of the necessary talents. We had all thought about the project a great deal, we had worked out many of the problems. *If* only ...!

Nothing directly was said to admit the defeat. We went on for a while communicating and planning, but now there was a slight air of fantasy about it all, something which had definitely not been present before. Possibly one or two of our distant members sensed this, for they began writing to us more regularly pressing us to hold further meetings, have a general get-together. At the time we staved off these requests for a while by telling the truth, that we were waiting for the long-promised on-the-spot report from young John Brooks, who by now we fondly imagined had been trudging manfully through the eight-foot weeds, focusing his cine camera on various aspects of our community site.

When, some months after we had first hoped for it, the letter finally came it somehow symbolized the whole rather sad and sorry story of our community venture. It was enormously long, about fifty hand-written pages, and full of fascinating detail – but in fact its purpose was to explain to us the almost ludicrous way in which John Brooks had *not* visited Great Barrier island after all! He had made all his plans and arranged about transport and so on, and then on the very day before he was due to go he was booked by his captain for some minor misdemeanour, as a result of which his leave was curtailed – and his trip had to be cancelled. As he rightly said it was utterly exasperating after all the preparations. As some kind of compensation he had accumulated a mass of information about the island from people who had been there and officials familiar with the terrain. What he had to say confirmed much of what we had felt instinctively, both as to the island's magical possibilities – and its rather grim limitations.

It became increasingly obvious to Jess and myself that we would be unable to make the final commitment. Through force of circumstances the Mosses had to call a halt, too, for the time being. At last we circularized the other interested parties and stated the position. Fortunately by now there were others prepared to go on with the scheme a little further. The Courts, at Brighton, had decided they really would go ahead and it was agreed that Hugh Court should take over the organization. At once, indeed, he made progress, too, for being more centrally situated he was able to make contacts much more easily.

One afternoon I gathered together all the masses of documents and booklets and reports we had accumulated in our New Zealand Community file, and wrapped them up in a large parcel to be sent off to the Courts. At the very top of the parcel was the roughly drawn pen and ink map of Great Barrier Island which the agent had sent us in response to our first inquiry. Jess and I sat and looked at it rather sadly, following the lines that marked the boundaries of our 'property', with the little marks that indicated the copper mine, the native bush, the reclaimable swamp, the hot springs, the amphibious landing place ... It was very much like looking at what might have been. It was already like looking at something out of a story-book. Yet there had been a time when we fully intended to go. Perhaps some day ... sadly, we finished wrapping our parcel, and posted it off with our good wishes to the new organizers.

VIII

Of Porches and Paintings and Pianos

As winter slowly moved towards spring and it seemed we were going to be lucky enough to escape the really bad weather up-country Jess and I would spend hours working out in the grounds. Her work was more constructive, planting and tending her garden. For my part I concentrated on a daily quota of sawing logs and storing them in a huge pile under cover as an insurance for future fires. Sawing is one of those pastimes I have always enjoyed, there is a curious satisfaction in gathering together such an asset. Wherever possible we only used trees that had either fallen down or were dead – now that we had Dutch elm disease more and more of the latter had been making their appearance obvious by the lack of any sort of growth.

Usually I would do my sawing in the afternoon, working on a bench outside the pottery workshop and a few feet from the gurgling river stream. Now and then I would pause for a breath of air, or to look up at the distant sound of a car that might be coming to our house (though it was much more likely to be bound for our neighbour). As I stood there, saw in hand, looking around at my domain, I would find myself sometimes suddenly remembering my very first glimpse of the Mill House, that sunny summer day when I rushed over after a call from the estate agent, parked my car outside the then firmly closed gate, and looked up the long drive.

The first sign of life I saw then was exactly the picture which I now formed – an elderly gentleman with a saw in his hand cutting up logs! This was Mr Main, the previous owner, who along with his wife had spent nearly thirty years at the

Mill House, and he and his wife, I feel sure, were very much in
the back to nature tradition. I always felt it must have seemed
very sad that old age made it necessary for them to move to the
greater convenience of a town house. Now, on this sunny and
careless afternoon, I felt the first far off prickings of my own
awareness that one day perhaps I, too, might have to think on
such terms. But not, thank goodness, yet awhile – and also,
even if we do have to move, the house will remain with the
family, and will always buzz and hum, I hope with the sound
of children's voices, another generation and another life going
on and on as it does, despite all our worldly madnesses.

When I was not steadily sawing up logs at the Mill House I
was quite likely, every afternoon, to be engaged (sometimes
rather morosely) on a project. I use the word carefully as it is
basically an euphemism for some task which I have been
challenged to do by an irate wife with a very low opinion of my
practical abilities. At this particular time the question had
cropped up yet again about building a small porch at the front
of the house in the forlorn hope we might then manage to
reduce the amount of dirt and wet brought in by people
stepping straight off the muddy drive outside. For some reason
which I was later to regret I conceived the idea that putting up
a porch might be one of those long term tasks which might
well suit my admittedly limited talents. After all I could handle
the ubiquitous Cornish breeze blocks which would form the
main base: after that it would seem to be simply a question of
building a two by two frame above, inserting some large glass
windows – and hey presto, a porch.

It was not, it became apparent, going to be quite as simple.
As was my wont I rushed into my new work with ferocious
enthusiasm: there being insufficient blocks to hand I had no
compunction in darting all over the place, stealing a couple
from Demelza's caravan, some more from another half
finished edifice somewhere, even taking three more which
enabled visitors to climb up into my own office. I didn't care
where I got them so long as I could assemble them outside the
front door and begin the task of setting them up in rows, with
cement of course. Here I committed my first gaffe, forgetting

the need to break up some blocks into halves so as to spread
them out in different patterns. Only when I had erected four
rows did a caustic Jess come along, give a scornful push, and
knock down my wall.

This was the first move in what became a running battle, a
rather sorry affair altogether. Herself a practical person, Jess
could not understand how a 62-year-old man of some worldly
experience was not efficient in putting up a simple thing
like a wall. I for my part found her attitude harsh and
unsympathetic. We both fell to reflecting sourly upon our total
incompatability even after (perhaps because of) thirty-one
years of marriage. This I suppose is one of the classic
syndromes of married life and comes of living too closely in
each other's pockets. In vain did I attempt to point out that
when Jess attempted to type her efforts were pathetic and that
this was simply a similar example, the other way round. My
protests cut no ice. Doggedly I went on rebuilding my wall –
angrily and contemptuously Jess kept either pointing out its
defects, or even in exasperation pushing it over again.

Meantime, in my first flush of enthusiasm I had rung up a
building firm over at Hayle and ordered 50 concrete blocks, a
quantity of sand, some cement, and about 90 feet of two by
two planking. Just when both Jess and I had had about our
worst row and decided to chuck the whole business an
enormous open lorry arrived at the bottom of our drive full of
the goods I had ordered. As always with lorries of all shapes
and sizes which venture down our lane the driver was already
in a state of considerable harassment, convinced not merely
that he would never be able to turn round but also that he
would never get out of the lane again. In the end, by some
exhausting manoeuvres, the man managed to back his lorry
right up to the front of the house and proceeded to tip up the
back and empty the blocks down all over our drive. Next the
wood planks were handed down, and then, breathing heavily
and no doubt offering up a prayer, the driver set off on his
somewhat nightmarish journey back along the narrow lane.

Well, since the materials were there, I reflected, I might as
well resume my onslaught – and this I did. As February

turned into March, and the first whiffs of Cornish spring filled
the air – we had already enjoyed our first golden daffodils
spread around like a magic carpet – Jess and I began going on
a few expeditions. I fear we are not very enterprising, unlike
my son Martin who carefully maps out walks from the
Ordnance survey: usually it is either a walk out along the
cliffs at Logan Rock, or at Porthgwarra, or an exhilarating
scamper over the wind-blown sands at Sennen Cove – or
perhaps, now and then a wander over at Zennor or St Ives. I
often feel guilty that we do not go further afield, to the Lizard,
or perhaps inland to Gweek, or across the other coast to
Gwithian and Hell's Mouth – heavens, what a variety
Cornwall has to offer. However I remind myself that at least in
the past I *have* covered Cornwall pretty extensively, and there
are not many corners or crannies which I have not visited at
some time or other.

I was reminded about all this when I called in one afternoon
on Margo Maeckleberghe to help choose a painting suitable
as a cover for my novel *Karenza*. For the first of my novels
which Peter Kimber published, *Barbican's End*, we had been
lucky enough to find one of Margo's Atlanta paintings that
was absolutely perfect. This time I could not believe that we
would be so lucky; at the same time the novel was once again
strongly Cornish in atmosphere, and I knew no painter who
has captured this feeling down here more vividly than Margo
– as indeed she proceeded to demonstrate by showing me at
least two dozen paintings that were bewildering in their light
and intensity and feeling. One of the things that draws me
almost irresistibly to Margo's paintings is precisely their
element of feeling, of movement; that is to say, though they are
landscapes or seascapes, they are *living* ones, you can almost
feel the granite writhing and twisting, just as you can actually
see the sea foaming and frothing. What's more, in most of the
paintings there is always an element of the unknown, of
mystery – a part left, almost one might say, unfinished.

We had a fascinating hour that afternoon ruminating about
the various paintings – was this one too bright, this one too
dim, would this green put off the reader, what about the

yellow – wasn't that eye-catching? Margo told me that she had found that almost every picture she had painted with a yellow in it had sold, so this obviously was something to bear in mind. Then again, though, we were torn between vertical paintings, which could only occupy the front page of a cover, and horizontal ones which might be used to spread around front and back – a most effective form of presentation if it comes off.

In the end, we managed to whittle down the choice to four paintings, of most striking sea and land views, full of movement and mystery. Since my novel was based on a theme concerning a young girl whose mind has been twisted by her mother drowning, and who is heading inexorably for a similar fate, we both felt that one of the magnificent and moving seascapes might be the best subject for the cover. On the other hand there was another view of the coast that also captured much of the mystery of the story. By the time this book appears the question will have long been settled and the book in the shops – but either way, thank you, Margo, for so adorning my novel.

Most of the books which I write, or indeed which any author writes I imagine, tend to be lonely affairs. That is why I welcome any chance of a little cooperation, as with Margo over those covers, or with Donald Swan who does the covers of my autobiographies. Editing, too, gives an opportunity for a sense of sharing in a common venture.

Sometimes I am amazed at the sheer number of books that have appeared on Cornwall: doing a quick count in our local library the other day I reached a figure of 400, and that is but a fraction of the true total. And still they come! What's more they come in quality and profoundly, not just in quantity. Only recently I have marvelled at such beautiful productions as the selection of famous photographs of shipwrecks on the Isles of Scilly, with an introduction by John Fowles, while not long ago my old friend Frank Baker, in his *The Call of Cornwall*, added yet another delightful original to the endless Cornish mystery. I have the feeling that with the appearance of my own new one, *The Spirit of Cornwall* I may have done enough direct writing on Cornwall, but of course the feeling and sense of the place will inevitably pervade everything I write, whether stories or novels or even articles and talks. It is impossible, as I shall never tire of saying, to live in Cornwall and remain unaffected. It is, indeed, the timeless land.

Of course, as I have tried to show in my autobiographical books, life in Cornwall is not all craggy cliffs and mysterious moors, nor confined to seas cascading over rocky shores – though all this is the stuff of drama, indeed. For those of us who live here, especially when we live in outlandish conditions, even the mundane things of everyday life can become quite colourful.

Take, for instance, the 'ongoing' story of the pianos in my life and the often bizarre circumstances of their acquisition and disposal. One of my first and most vivid memories is of a time soon after Jess and I, along with a growing brood of children (three down, one on the way), had moved into our tall terrace house in Morrab Place, Penzance. It was the very first house of our own, bought thanks to a combination of my mother and a local building society, and we hadn't much money to spare for furniture. In those days you could pick up bargains at local auction sales so we used to go along. Unfortunately on one occasion I omitted to go along – whereas Jess did and got so excited that she bid £12.50 for an absolutely enormous grand piano. Of course what we really wanted were tables and chairs and beds – but here we were landed with probably the biggest piano in the whole of the West Country. At the end of the sale there was nothing for it, since we couldn't afford a removal van, but to wheel the damn thing down through the main street of Penzance to our new home.

Monstrosity is the only word to describe that grand piano upon whose spacious veneered top you could comfortably have spread a double bed (why didn't I think of that!). The piano was so big we could only get it into the facing ground floor room used as my 'study'. Once in it dominated all life to such an extent that in order to reach my desk I had to either climb over the piano or crawl under it. From the beginning I had a fairly understandable psychological dislike of the piano, refusing to play a note and generally nagging Jess until she was stung into declaring bitterly: 'Well, you needn't worry – the wood alone is worth more than I paid.' Amazingly she was right and a young furniture maker was glad to come along and pay us £15 on the spot.

After that piano memories proliferate. When soon after we moved from Penzance out to Peter's Cottage, our romantic home on the cliffs near Land's End, I remember vividly a group of us manhandling an old upright down the cliff path, every now and then pausing to take breath – or rather have it punched down into our lungs by a 90 mile an hour Atlantic gale. Once or twice I feared the piano might take off and land down in Sennen Cove, but somehow we got it down into the snug granite cottage. At least the kids got some fun out of tinkling at the keys – myself I was too busy listening uneasily to the howling winds and the whistling gales and wondering if the house would survive the winter, let alone the piano.

When next we moved to the Old Vicarage 'up country' – that is, in Cornish terms, five miles or so to the other side of Penzance – we left the old piano, unable to face the task of carrying it up the steep cliff. By then we were into that golden period when pianos were out of favour and you could buy one for two or three pounds. People were even giving them away and I think our next one was such a present. Like most of our pianos it came of pretty nondescript mongrel stock, but it did experience one supreme moment of glory. This was on the occasion of our annual Boxing Night Party when, under the influence of a particularly potent rum punch, several of our friends decided they would move not only the party but the piano too from our sitting room across the wide hall and out into the cold night air and then up a steep flight of stairs leading into the studio then occupied by our friend Donald Swan. In no time at all the piano was settled in a corner among half finished canvasses, a somewhat inebriated honky tonk expert was placed on the stool and told to start playing – and soon a long line of us were swaying round the studio in a creditable imitation of the Conga.

Pianos kept coming and going in our lives, especially during the decade when we lived in that low rambling old house overlooking Porthmeor Beach, St Ives. It was a marvellous setting for family life and I once wrote a whole book about it called *The Door is Always Open*, describing our bitter and indeed regular experiences of the sea flooding the downstairs floor. Fortunately the pianos always seemed to escape damage, which was just as well as by then we had become quite a musical family, often in the evenings having a real family band going, myself on the piano, Demelza on the drum set, and Stephen on his guitar, with one or two occasional singing gate-crashers. Somewhere there is a faded tape recording of one of these sessions and say what you like I find something rather endearing about those hesitant, fluctuating tinkling sounds of – wait for it, yes, you've guessed – 'Red Sails in the Sunset', 'Smoke Gets in Your Eyes', etc. Our St Ives pianos hadn't much character but one of them provided a suitably grandiose sacrifice for one Guy Fawkes Night – being bodily hurled on top of a huge bonfire half way down the beach.

Undoubtedly the most remarkable interlude in our life with pianos came when we went to live at the Old Sawmills, that romantic old mill house set on the edge of the River Fowey, so remote that it could only be reached by boat. I shall never forget the time (now part of the folklore of the local village at Golant) when with the inevitable upright piano standing in state in the centre of a dangerously-low-in-the-water dinghy Stephen and I cautiously set off down river towards the creek where our new home stood in all its glory. The River Fowey can be tricky on an incoming tide – even trickier when the tide has turned and begins racing down to the sea. Nevertheless, because of the obvious difficulties posed by attempting to row against a powerful incoming tide we had chosen to risk embarking with our precious load just *after* the tide turned. This meant that rowing was no problem but guiding the boat, especially turning it out of the river and into our creek in the face of a powerful current – well, that threatened to be a disaster.

Stephen and I had no time for words. We stood upright, one

at the bow and one at the stern (we couldn't have sat, anyway, the piano took all the room), our eyes glued upon that narrow opening into the creek. I waited anxiously until Stephen, officially captain of our tiny vessel for the occasion, shouted out in a strangled voice: 'Now!' – and then with the two of us rowing like mad we just about edged the boat under the tiny bridge and into the more placid waters of the creek. Of course by waiting until the tide was going out we ran the risk of there not being enough water for our dinghy to reach the little quay ... and indeed, needless to say, we ran aground in squelching mud about twenty feet off. Now we faced a new danger for as the water melted away leaving us high and dry the dinghy and its unnatural top-heavy load began to tilt over further and further. For some time we were both too petrified to move in case the piano went overboard and disappeared forever beneath the clinging soft mud.

Fortunately both dinghy and piano remained seaborne and in due course when the tide came in again, we accomplished the further difficult task of carrying the piano up an incline of thirty steps, finally and breathlessly depositing it in our little sitting room overlooking creek and woods. There it remained a year or two until, as is the way with most of our pianos, it simply wilted away and we had to find a replacement. This time we thought we would be clever, so we borrowed a friend's launch and Stephen towed the dinghy and piano down river – which seemed a bright idea until just as he was about to swing into the creek, the tow rope snapped.

Our last sight of Stephen, the piano and the dinghy was of the whole lot being swept at about seven knots straight towards the china clay docks, narrowly missing collisions with two incoming and probably rather startled cargo steamers. The strange boatload was remorselessly carried on past Fowey and Polruan and was nearly out in the open sea before the harbour-master's launch chugged up and managed to effect a rescue.

After these sort of experiences the move to our present home would appear to encourage a quiet life, piano-wise – after all here you can drive a van to the front door and have a piano installed with no trouble. However the problems still seem to be around. Obviously envious of our piano in the main house Stephen, installed in his chalet in the grounds, got four or five hefty friends to help him carry a venerable old second-hand upright all the way up to his little home. Then, hardly was that installed, when an old friend of mine asked if we could possibly store for him a treasured and valuable old piano. Foolishly we agreed, realising when the piano arrived that there was nowhere to put it – in the end stacking it, with many misgivings, in an old garden hut. Here we hoped our friend's piano would be safe and sound, but alas a winter of Cornish gales and storms tore off the garden hut roof and – well, we just try and avoid the subject whenever we see our old friend.

So is this where our piano story reaches its triumphant finale? Er, not quite. Recently when we had the piano tuner out he pronounced our latest piano not worthy of repair. However as it happened he did know where there was a very good instrument going most reasonably, and if we liked he could get the owner to deliver it in his own van. And that's what happened. We called in Stephen and some of his hefty young friends to carry our original piano and store it in yet another outhouse – and in due course the new piano arrived and was installed. So now we have *four* pianos in our life. You think that's a lot? Well, just wait a moment. Having recently set up her caravan in a corner of the garden, Demelza has been doing measurements, and she's confident she can squeeze in *at least* a mini-piano. I rather fear she's just gone into town to order one from the local music shop ...

IX

Sailing Down the Shannon

When one day the large and glossy April issue of the magazine *Motor Boat and Yachting* appeared with our morning post, I was quite thrilled to find pride of place given to a very long and profusely illustrated article of my own on the theme 'Islands of the Mediterranean'. Make no mistake about it, no matter how long we writers have been writing, nor how often published, we always retain a kind of peacock pride in seeing our progeny in print. In this instance the appreciation was somewhat long overdue as I had sweated hard on that article about two years previously and recently had been wondering if it would ever see the light of day. However in the end I could hardly complain: it was magnificently presented with a whole series of colourful photographs, some of beauty spots we have visited, and quite a few of crew members of *Sanu* in what might be called working attitudes.

The real trouble about seeing the article was that it brought back such a flood of vivid memories that I could almost feel the gathering tears of regret – for, of course, this year was to see the end of *Sanu*'s long, long trip back from the Mediterranean to the white cliffs of England, or rather the granite ones of Cornwall. At such a time it was impossible not to feel haunted by feelings of sadness, at the end of an era. All right, maybe, a new one was going to start, but I must confess in my heart of hearts I viewed my impending nautical homecoming with very mixed feelings – and indeed more than once had been tempted to fly out to Portugal, turn *Sanu*'s bow east, and head back to the dear old Med! Be that as it may, for quite a while nothing would stop the endless flood of memories. After all, since we acquired *Sanu* about fifteen years back, together with most of our family Jess and I had had the great good fortune to travel to Germany, Denmark, Sweden, Ireland, France, Holland, Spain, Portugal, Italy, Malta, Greece, Turkey ... covering nearly 30,000 miles, visiting 12 sovereign countries, berthing in something like 300 separate ports or anchorages.

Looked at it in cold print, I can't help feeling this represents quite an achievement for a family which only a year or two before *Sanu* came into our life used to view a trip up the River Thames or a leisurely sail round the Norfolk Broads as the height of nautical adventure. In those days we used to have to hire boats for our family excursions, and as a way of learning to handle boats I can highly recommend it. Naturally the experience cannot quite be compared with adventures in a boat of your own – all the same before we came to the end of our rent-a-boat period we did embark on one water-borne holiday that could well stand up to most of our later adventures, as far as excitement and trauma are concerned. This was when Jess and I, with Stephen, Demelza and Genevieve, decided to widen our horizons by going to Ireland and hiring a large motor cruiser for a trip down the mighty River Shannon. Not only is the Shannon the longest river in the British Isles (214 miles) it also encompasses a series of loughs, many so large as to be virtually inland seas (the whole of the Norfolk Broads could be put into the largest, Lough Derg, which measures 24 miles long and covers 50 square miles – and Lough Ree is nearly as big, being 18 miles long and in some parts 3 miles across).

From the brightly coloured brochures we obtained we decided that this would certainly be a holiday with a difference as well as providing very useful nautical experience, so we arranged to hire a six berth motor cruiser, 35 feet long and with a diesel engine, and booked our flight from Exeter to Dublin. Ten hours precisely after leaving our home at St Ives we were on the quayside at a little riverside village, and there was our cruiser waiting. It wasn't quite as roomy as we had hoped but seemed quite comfortable.

Soon after arriving the owner of the boatyard – 'Himself' as he was always referred to by the staff, in the Irish way – gave us a somewhat Irish welcome by assuring us that everything was ready and then apologizing in the nicest possible way for the fact that the hot water system was not back from being repaired, and neither had the new sailing dinghy arrived. 'Sure, but we'll be after getting you a sailing dinghy in no time and we'll bring it down to you wherever you are.'

Jess – who all along had maintained that the holiday was a big mistake, and had positively grinned gleefully as the rain pelted down on the minibus journey (though now once more the sun was shining, thank goodness) – raised her eyebrows meaningfully, but I chose to ignore such defeatism. After all, these little things weren't important; there was a rowing dinghy anyway and everything else seemed to be in working order.

'Right,' I said, purposefully. 'We'll be making a start. I hope to get twenty miles down river this evening, ready for crossing Lough Ree tomorrow.'

Himself assured me that this was perfectly feasible, but he would just like to take me for a trial run to see that my boating ability was up to standard. He pressed the button and started the big diesel engine, and we headed off under the bridge for a short run up river. Himself meantime demonstrated the controls.

'It's really quite simple, as you'll be seeing. Oh ...!'

The last remark greeted the sudden and mysterious silencing of the engine. At once the boat began to drift in the grip of the swift current. Quickly Himself ran to the bow, loosened the anchor and threw it out, so that after a while the boat stopped drifting.

'That's very strange.'

'Yes,' I said, unhappily aware of Jess sitting with arms folded, expecting it all. 'It is, isn't it ... Can you make it go again?'

Miraculously, it seemed, after poking about a little, Himself did get the engine to go. He quickly pulled in the anchor and we set off again, this time heading down river towards the bridge and the boatyard.

'Oh, well,' I said, mainly for Jess's benefit, 'I suppose it was just some little thing. Well, we'll be off soon, eh?'

I became conscious of a curious constriction in Himself, at my side. Almost in a whisper he spoke in my ear.

'Now would you be minding if I made a suggestion? Would it be causing you any great inconvenience if you were to stay the night here after all? Would it now?'

Well, of course, it would, but some instinct warned me that there was some hidden meaning in that remark.

'Sure, you see, I'd like to just get a diesel mechanic along to check over the engine – just in case. You never know, now, do you? I'd feel much happier, indeed I would.'

So it was agreed. When Himself had departed to fetch a diesel mechanic – apparently they were as rare in Ireland as oases in the desert – Jess hunched up her shoulders expressively and went off to cook our first meal aboard – still tied up at the boatyard quay.

Quite late that evening, when the children were already snug in their bunks, the mechanic turned up along with Himself, and the two of them soon had the floorboards up and, by the light of a powerful torch, began examining the innards of the engine. As I expected one day to be needing to understand diesel engines myself, I watched with some fascination as the engine cover was taken off revealing a revolting gummy oily conglomeration of tappets and pistons and other mysterious working parts. It all looked beyond comprehension to me but the mechanic painstakingly checked all the various parts, and at the end shook his head. 'Twas a bit on the noisy side, he agreed – in that endearing Irish lilt that made every conversation in that country seem an extraordinarily romantic one even if it was just the purchase of a loaf of bread – but as far as he could tell it was all right.

'There, you see,' I said to Jess later, 'we've not really wasted any time, and now we can relax.'

In the morning, nicely relaxed, we got up early, had a quick breakfast, and prepared for our long awaited voyage. When all was ready I pressed the button and the engine immediately roared into life. Jess and Stephen cast off the mooring ropes and we set off downriver towards our first lock, about half a mile down. The lockkeeper there not only gave us a friendly wave, but his entire family came out to greet us, as apparently we were one of the first boats to be seen on the river that season. Like most locks I had passed through on rivers and canals, this one had a most pleasant and homely atmosphere, with a beautifully tended garden. For all its isolation, it seemed a delightful spot at which to live.

The lockkeeper and his son opened the far gates and – rather proud of my new craft – I steered the boat out into the broadening river. In some of my pre-trip reading I had noted that in most places the Shannon was as much as 300 yards wide, but it had not really registered. Now, as we purred away down river and the banks receded far to each side, I realized that it *was* a very wide river indeed: lonely, too, for all around us there was just rolling empty countryside, not a sign of any habitations. Yes, beautiful and lonely and ...

At that precise moment, the engine gave a pathetic flutter or two, and then died away completely. It was, I knew instinctively, a repetition of what had happened on the trial run. Hastily I ran along the deck and put out the anchor, for there was a strong current and otherwise in quite a short time our large boat would have been carried along and aground on the inhospitable looking barren banks. Then I went back to the cockpit and pressed the starter. There was a burring noise, and then a click. I pressed again. This time there was just a click, and silence. In my heart I knew that something was radically wrong, but hopelessly I went on pressing the starter.

Meantime my crew were becoming restive. Why didn't I start the engine? Surely I could make it go again? Probably it was a dirty plug or something. Last night the man had just waited a few moments and then got it going again. Why couldn't I?

Under the pressure of these derisive influences I began to lose control a little of my captain's cool, iron nerve. After all, I knew, if they didn't, that we were stranded in the middle of a huge river 300 yards wide, and it was time to hurry up about getting some help.

'There's nothing for it, I'll have to get in the dinghy and row back to that lock.'

Ignoring what I regarded as grossly unjust taunts of 'Mr Panic!' I hurried to the back of the boat, grabbed at the rope of the dinghy and hastily untied it from the holder. Unfortunately I had forgotten the very strong current which flows down the Shannon – for a fraction of a second my hand let go its grip on the rope, and in that brief span the dinghy suddenly swirled away from me.

'The dinghy – the dinghy! It's gone!'

Aghast, I pointed to where the dinghy was being carried away by the current, so that it must be forty or fifty feet down stream already.

'What on earth did you do that for?' demanded Jess.

I had no satisfactory answer. I could only hang my head in shame, as we contemplated the now greatly increased gravity of our position, stranded at anchor in the middle of a lonely river and without any means of getting to the shore.

'There's only one thing for it,' Jess turned briskly to her son, 'You'll have to swim to the dinghy. Come on, get your clothes off, Stephen.'

I wish I could do justice in words to the shades of expression which now fitfully crossed Stephen's face. Horror, outrage, indignation, self-pity, persecution, martyrdom – the whole gamut, from A to Z, were encompassed in a few moments. Nevertheless the fact remained he was the only one of us who was a good swimmer.

'Come on for God's sake, get your clothes off and into your costume.'

Somehow, but very unwillingly, Stephen began taking his clothes off, so slowly in fact that the dinghy was far out of reach of even a good swimmer by the time, shivering extravagantly, he made his appearance in a bathing costume.

'Idiot!' I said rather unkindly. 'You've left it too late. I tell you what: look, the dinghy's caught in some reeds. We'll get the anchor up and let our boat drift down until it's level with the dinghy, then you won't have far to swim.'

After much manoeuvring, that is precisely what we did.

When we were level with the dinghy, about 50 yards away, we re-anchored our boat, and then wearing a lifebelt round his neck as an added precaution, Stephen dived off the boat and swam towards the dinghy. It wasn't very far really, but it was a brave effort – one incidentally we had the presence of mind to take on a cine camera for imperishable records. When he finally reached the dinghy and, with some difficulty pulled himself aboard, we all gave three rousing cheers.

Grinning broadly Stephen rowed back to the boat, and then I took over, and hastily began rowing the dinghy back up stream. Going against the current it took me quite a long time to reach the lock, where they were naturally surprised to see me. With that kindness which we found a truly universal characteristic of the Irish the lockkeeper told his son to drive me back to the boatyard and about an hour after we set off so proudly, I was knocking at the workshop door. The foreman appeared and listened to my story sympathetically.

'Ah, dear, and isn't it a pity? Himself has gone off to Carrick. But he'll be back any time, don't you worry.'

'But Carrick must be, why, twenty miles or more?'

'Sure, and I suppose it is. But he'll be back soon, don't you worry.'

At that stage in our Irish holiday, I was not wholly conversant with Irish ideas of time, and for an hour or so I stood impatiently waiting for the miraculous re-appearance of Himself. Then, beginning to fear the worst, I forced the foreman and his mate to get out a spare boat and take me back down river, where we got a rope on the big boat and laboriously managed to tow her back into the safety of the lock. At least that meant my family weren't liable to float away to God knows where.

All that afternoon I stood grimly by the side of the foreman at the boatyard trying to will the appearance of help in some shape or another. As yet another exasperation it transpired that the boatyard's own mechanic was away in London for a wedding – I had been assured he would be back on the next train from Dublin, but in fact he never appeared either that day or even the next. At last, wilting under my ceaseless demands the foreman agreed to send for the same diesel mechanic who had spent half the previous evening on our boat. I went back to the lock, where Jess was now icy and silent and the children morose and miserable, and we all sat and waited.

Around early evening there arrived both the diesel mechanic and a friend, and Himself, back at last from his trip up river. He was most eloquent in sympathy for our predicament – ' 'Tis the last thing I would have wanted to happen, indeed.' He then produced an alternative suggestion – namely that we should have a four-berth boat, towing the speedboat, in turn towing the rowing boat – which almost gave Jess apoplexy. Hastily Himself agreed that perhaps in the circumstances the fairest thing would be to refund us our money. Perhaps we would like to hire a car and go for a motor tour of the Irish countryside?

At that stage, mentally and emotionally exhausted, I thought it wise to remove a rather stony Jess from this upsetting atmosphere. It was agreed that Himself would see to hiring a car, meantime the three children went off for a row in the dinghy and, cravenly, I propelled Jess across the bridge to what I discovered was one of seven separate bars serving a total of fifty inhabitants. As it happened this one was run by the same lively gentleman who had supplied us with our grocery supplies, the previous evening. Now in the course of serving us with several life giving rums and brandies, he bestowed on us a free flow of that marvellous Irish blarney which we discovered to be almost commonplace in the land. At the end of an hour Jess obviously felt much better, and both of us had acquired a certain mellowness, as compared to our former irritability.

This was just as well, for when we got back to the quayside we found lined up a determined looking deputation of three resolute children.

'We don't want to drive about Ireland in a car! We want to go on the River Shannon. We *won't* go in a car!'

Since this was still very much my own desire, I fear that Jess was left in a pronounced minority. Meantime Himself had arrived back, having tentatively fixed up a car. I explained the new change of mind, and he at once made a new offer.

'Sure, and would you not be liking *two* four-berth boats? Your wife could be in charge of one, and you the other, and there's plenty of berths for you all.'

So it came about that two days later than we intended, and in two boats instead of one, we finally set off on our long-awaited cruise down the River Shannon. Demelza and Genevieve were with me in the leading boat, and Jess and Stephen followed behind. It seemed a reasonable enough solution; there had not been time yet for me to discover how very exhausting it was going to be for me as the solitary skipper of my craft, without any relief in the steering – in the other boat, Jess and Stephen at least could take turns.

However, all went well the first day. We made about twenty miles down the winding river to reach Lanesborough, a market town which marked the entrance to the first of our formidable lakes, Lough Ree. Here I regret to say we made a rather ignoble exhibition of ourselves, though not entirely through our own fault. When turning my boat to come up at a quay the engine suddenly failed and there was such an angry strong current flowing down that in no time at all I found myself slewed across the low arch of Lanesborough Bridge, with the bow against one pillar and the stern against another, and a 6-knot tide trying to force the boat through the bridge! With the engine defunct and resisting all attempts to start again I was completely helpless.

After a while Jess and Stephen brought their boat round to try and tow us off but the tide was so strong that for one horrific period they, too, were jammed against us! In the end they managed to tie a rope, and finally we were towed to safety. Through all this brief, nightmarish experience we were watched with supercilious amusement by a party of pure yachting types whose eyes I carefully avoided as we finally pulled in at the quay.

Fortunately there was nothing seriously wrong with the engine, and the next morning we prepared for the crossing of Lough Ree. I was not happy for two reasons. First, the weather was really bad, great grey clouds and choppy waters, and whenever Stephen and I took a walk on Lanesborough Bridge to have a look out on the Lough all we could see were dreaded white horsemen waves – obviously we would have to wait a while before embarking. The second reason for unease was my *Shannon Guide* comments:

> Lough Ree should be treated with respect. In strong winds, particularly from the north-west, it becomes very rough, the seas being short and steep. In many places there is little sea room and waves must be taken as they come, as often as not on the beam. The lake is difficult in bad light or misty weather as some of the important markers are over two miles apart. Even in clear weather binoculars are helpful ... Off the marked course there are very many unmarked shoals and isolated rocks ... Exploring is only safe for those who can really navigate.

It was perhaps a little unfortunate that shortly after re-reading the *Guide* for the umpteenth time I went outside and found a strange motor-cruiser just being berthed. I went over to it and found a man, somewhat eccentrically clad in a dressing-gown, at the wheel. When he turned and looked at me I was startled to see that his eyes had a glazed, almost haunted look. I began to ask a question which suddenly seemed unnecessary – quite obviously he *had* just brought his boat across Lough Ree in the very roughest kind of weather, and he was still in a traumatic state. When he recovered a little, he began indicating with huge gestures of his arms the size of the waves, and shaking his head as if in wonder at his escape.

Stephen and I wandered away, somewhat disconsolate. Still, we felt we could hardly stay at Lanesborough day after day – especially as, having noted the extraordinary number of garages (we counted six in one street) when we went to buy some petrol the man shook his head and said, 'Ah, now, sure but the petrol won't be in till tomorrow.' Best really be on our way, we could get petrol the other side of the lake.

So, encouraged by spasmodic sunshine after lunch, at last

we set off. I had noted grimly that unlike most other parts of
the river, Lough Ree offered no havens of refuge. Once we set
off, we had the whole eighteen miles to cover before we
reached the one safe quayside, at Hodson's Bay. At first it
seemed as if the waves had quietened down a bit, but after
going a few miles and emerging into the really wide parts of
the Lough (often more than three miles wide, just like an
inland sea) we soon found ourselves caught in a choppy sea,
and our 26-foot motor-boats began tossing about like corks. I
found that indeed it was necessary to take the waves on the
beam, just as stated in the *Guide*, which did not help. Beside
me in the cockpit Demelza and Genevieve looked rather
alarmed, as was not surprising: just to be safe I made them
put on their life belts, and concentrating grimly on what now
seemed an interminable journey. Every now and then I looked
over my shoulder to make sure my sister ship was dutifully
following, thinking to myself that perhaps it was just as well I
could not hear Jess's comments. But most of the time I was
peering intently forward, for it was indeed often very difficult
to pick up the red or black buoys which marked the passage –
especially when after half an hour a rainstorm fell upon us, so
that I could hardly see the sea, let alone the buoys!

It was a really rough crossing, and I heaved an enormous
sigh of relief when finally, two hours later, I sighted the red
buoy that marks the entrance into Hodson's Bay, where we
finally moored up at a neat little sheltered quay. We had read
avidly in the guide book that at Hodson's Bay there was a
pleasant hotel where baths were readily provided for boating
parties – and low and behold, every word was true. What's
more, we all ate a really stupendous meal at the hotel in the
evening, as a change from the severe limitations of Calor gas
cooking, at sea.

When we came out afterwards the sky had cleared
completely and there was a marvellous sunset over the wide
expanse of lakes. Stephen got out the dinghy and briskly
rowed over to a strange little island, on top of which stood a
simple granite stone. While we were filming his trip on the
camera a local boat owner came over and said to me: 'That's

supposed to be the centre of Ireland, you know.' So Stephen can boast an uncommon achievement.

It was about the first moment we had really been able to relax and I think in many ways from then on we really began to appreciate the often breathtaking beauty of the Irish countryside, particularly around the lakes. On Lough Ree, for instance, there were no fewer than fifty-two named islands and many smaller ones. Many were attractively wooded, and nine were inhabited – including one, Inchcleraun, where it is believed Queen Maeve went bathing 2,000 years ago, and was murdered by an enemy using a sling from the eastern shore. On this as on some of the other islands, there are ruins of very ancient churches, apparently there was a greater concentration of followers of St Patrick in Lough Ree than anywhere else in Ireland.

Fortified by our night at Hodson's Bay, we passed on the next day to Athlone, a pleasant large town in the centre of the country, and then followed the winding thirty-five miles down the Shannon towards Portumna, and Lough Derg. It was during this part of the trip that we spent a fascinating lunch time visiting the famous ruins, at Clonmacnois, of a great monastic city of ancient times, including examples of the round towers to be found in other parts of Ireland. It is a lonely wind-swept spot, commanding extensive views over surrounding bog-lands, and it was impossible to wander about the ruins without feeling a tremendous haunting sense of the past – an impression greatly enhanced by the remarkable collection of some 500 early grave-slabs, still bearing carved inscriptions in Irish and Latin. We discovered that these dated from the seventh to the eleventh centuries; some were ornamental as well as inscribed, the usual opening words being *Oriot*, 'a prayer for ...'

We had moored at a pontoon landing stage at Clonmacnois and when the time came to leave again we found the river had become quite choppy from the strong wind blowing on to the shore. In order to get away smartly from the pontoon we revved up our engines and set off at full power. Jess and Stephen went first, and we followed them in a great sweep and headed down river, feeling rather pleased with our quick getaway. Suddenly, however, my smugness was broken by an anguished cry from Genevieve.

'The dinghy! Daddy, quick, look – the dinghy!'

For the second (and not the last) time that trip I had the mortification of watching our dinghy rapidly disappearing away from its mother boat. What must have happened was that in swinging away sharply from the bank we had omitted to allow enough space for the trailing dinghy – witness to its abrupt severance was the piece of torn rope dangling from our stern. This time at least we had the engine going and were able, after some quite difficult manoeuvres, to grab the bow of the dinghy with a boat-hook and refasten the rope. But it was yet another of a series of niggling incidents that conspired always to keep us in a perpetual sense of unease as we went on down the winding river on what was to be our longest single day's journey, a matter of about thirty-five miles from Athlone to Portumna, gateway to Lough Derg.

It was such a long journey in fact that we began to think it would never end, particularly when, five miles from Portumna, we came to our last lock, Meelick, to find the lock-keeper away at a funeral and his wife, half-crippled with arthritis, unable to operate the lock. Fortunately Stephen and I had had a good deal of experience with locks on the Welsh canals, and we persuaded the lock-keeper's wife to lend us the ratchets, and laboriously worked the lock ourselves. It was a very deep fall, about twelve feet, and it involved at the end a precarious descent down a ladder to the roof of our boats, but we managed. That night we spent snug in the canal at Portumna, ready for our assault on the biggest of all the Shannon lakes.

Lough Derg is the largest and most dangerous of the Shannon Lakes. On the main navigation westerly winds can produce a confused sea shorter and steeper than anything encountered in coastal waters. In the days of commercial traffic harbours of refuge were constructed on the lake. Here barges sheltered when caught out on the

lake, and these harbours are still the only safe anchorages.
Take great care when navigating this large area of water.

Everything in the *Guide*, we were to discover, was almost an
understatement. Maybe at the height of summer Lough Derg
is as smooth and calm as a sheet of glass, but during our two
days on its turbulent waters we might well have been out at
sea. For our first trip we headed half-way down to a refuge
called Kilgarvan Quay – a place so expertly tucked away in
the wooded coastline that we had to traverse up and down two
or three times before at last we spotted the faint red buoy
marking the opening. By then the waves were whipping up
and we were glad to pull in at one of the old barge quays.
Shortly afterwards we were joined by some RAF men who
were canoeing their way from the source of the Shannon to the
sea end – two of them drove ahead each day in a van and set
up camp, another pair brought down the canoe. It hardly
surprised us to learn, later that day, that their canoe had
encountered tremendous rough seas and the occupants had
been lucky to beach it further up river, and hitch-hike down. It
was that sort of day, and we were glad to spend it, and the
night, in that sheltered haven.

The next morning the weather was not much better, but
studying the *Guide* I set my eyes on Garrykennedy Harbour,
on the southern stretch which 'gives perfect shelter', and
decreed that we must get there before lunch-time.

The journey to Garrykennedy was quite rough, but
nothing, did we but know it, to what was to come. It was such
a tiny harbour that again we found some difficulty in locating
it, but once there we were charmed – it really was snug and
sheltering, and the village delightfully picturesque. I was
immediately drawn to a loquacious old fisherman who took
our rope when we landed, and told me some of his experiences
during thirty years on the lake. Even now he was in the middle
of building a boat of his own, painstakingly and lovingly. He
was a completely contented and happy man, reflected in his
personality all that was best in the Irish. In his world, one felt,
the scale of values was properly adjusted, time had no special

meaning; the days came and the days went, you were alone with the sky and the sun and the waters, enveloped in a sort of timeless peace.

It was tempting to spend the rest of the day at Garrykennedy, but I was worried about getting fuel and water, which I knew were available at Killaloe, at the southern end of the lake. Besides, we were due to start back the next day; it would be sensible to make Killaloe that evening. Anxiously we kept watching the sky. I had to admit it was not encouraging. Momentarily it would clear and the sun would shine brightly, but almost immediately along the line of the horizon would build up an alarming thick wad of white clouds – soon these would spread all over the sky, turning a dark grey, and there would be a sudden venomous squall. On the radio Jess heard a gale warning broadcast for the Shannon area. I pointed out that applied to the sea entrance, but obviously Jess was not convinced. She was, indeed, all for staying at Garrykennedy and never going anywhere again in a boat! However, in the late afternoon the weather appeared to modify – there was even a rainbow (which later I heard was regarded as a *bad* sign in those parts!).

Finally the skipper of another cruiser boat which was waiting in the harbour to go on up river said he had decided to go on, as the weather seemed better. Could I move our boats so that he could get out of the harbour? I looked at the sky: it was suddenly quite clear, only the faintest of white clouds on the horizon. It was only ten miles round the point to Killaloe. If we went now, it would only take an hour ...

'Right!' I said, trying to sound masterful and determined. 'We'll be off, too. Cast off, Stephen – come on, look lively.'

As I spoke I tried to avoid looking at the tide outside the harbour, which was still flowing past with remarkable velocity – tried also to forget how a woman in one of the cottages had told me that when we rounded Parker Point we would encounter a swell three times as bad as at Garrykennedy. So be it, it would all be over in an hour, our boats were quite seaworthy, no good to worry.

We had hardly got out of the harbour and headed south-west when, with a sinking heart, I recognized ahead a vast increase in the number of white horses on the waves. Almost immediately the boat began rearing and tossing as it had done in the worst of Lough Ree – only somehow this time, I sensed, things were going to be even worse. Sure enough, after half a mile the swell had deepened so that the boat was rising right up out of the water and crashing down. At one such moment, unbeknown to us for a little while, the dinghy rope must have snapped again. When finally we noticed, the dinghy was a hundred yards behind us and the sea so rough that, on my own without anyone to help, I did not dare try to turn our boat, for the waves would have been broadside and might well have turned us over.

'The dinghy! The dinghy!' screamed Demelza.

I shook my head firmly.

'Never mind the dinghy – put your lifebelts on,' I paused. 'And hand me mine!'

It was the only time on the trip I wore my lifebelt, but I certainly felt likely to need it. As soon as we reached the exposed water around the Point we encountered the full force of a raging sea whipped up by the wind over a three mile stretch from Scariff, in the west. Our relatively small boats were seized and hurled up and then smacked down; sometimes the bow was several feet in the air, a moment later it was plunged down and the waves were spattering all over the cockpit. I could hardly blame the two girls for being thoroughly frightened. I was myself, but at least I was fully occupied hanging grimly on to the wheel and trying to keep the head of the boat into the waves. On Lough Ree, this had been impossible because we were forced to take a course that left us broadside on – if this had been so here I doubt if we would have survived, but fortunately we were heading all the time into the waves. Even so it was quite terrifying, especially as the coast on either side looked most inhospitable, jagged rocks and barren looking fields sloping up to mountains, not a sign of life anywhere.

Every now and then we looked back and saw Jess and Stephen's boat a hundred yards behind, performing the most extraordinary gyrobatics, at which we would have laughed at any other time – but not now, especially when we realized that this was just how our own boat must look to an observer.

The ordeal, for suddenly it had become such, seemed never-ending. Every few moments the tossing of the boat would loosen the engine cover and it would tumble off – meaning that the engine was liable to get a spray of water from the next heavy sea – and either Demelza or Genevieve had to crawl along the floor and replace it, since I dare not leave the wheel. However, I'm thankful to say, the powerful little Volvo-Penta engine never faltered, and boomed away even though sometimes the propeller was right out of the water!

At last we saw ahead of us the large black buoy that marked the entrance to the narrower channel leading to Killaloe: once we were past that, I felt, we would have taken the worst of the sea. Alas, the buoy seemed to stay permanently out of reach, and the boat tossed up and down, up and down, spray crashing over us. Would we never get level? At last, miraculously, we did – and past it. Almost at once the waves began to slacken; probably it was still quite rough, but by comparison with what we had been through for the past three-quarters of an hour it almost seemed calm.

I breathed a long drawn sigh of relief, as we headed down the narrowing channel for Killaloe. Then:

'Look, Dad – quick. Something's wrong with Jess's boat. They're stopped! Oh, Dad, turn round!'

Startled I looked round to see that the other boat had indeed slowed down. I couldn't make out what was wrong, so made a slow turn and headed back. However, before we reached them there was a spurt of movement and they came on, obviously all right again, so I turned and went on ahead.

It was ten minutes later when Demelza said in a puzzled way.

'Doesn't Jess's boat look funny?'

It did indeed. What was the matter? Somehow, though heading after us, the boat seemed to be sheering sideways ... Ah yes, it was clear now – it was tilting over, that was it. One side was higher than the other, quite pronouncedly.

'They're sinking! They're sinking!'

I looked intently. Something was radically wrong, undoubtedly, but the boat was still coming along at a fair pace. I looked ahead, and saw, thankfully, the distant outline of Killaloe, and, nearer still, the quay where the petrol pumps and water supplies were to be had. There was only one thing for it now, we must get there as quickly as possible.

Our own boat had survived the ordeal very well, fortunately, and a few moments later we had tied up at the quay, and jumped ashore to watch for Jess's arrival. Her boat certainly looked odder and odder! It was settling lower in the water – what could have happened? About 50 yards out we heard the engine suddenly peter out, and there was a shout – which meant, in effect, that they no longer could control her coming in. We did our best to fend her off, but the prow of the boat drove straight into the corner of our stern and caused a large gaping hole.

This however, it transpired, was merely a minor item compared with what had happened. As soon as we climbed aboard Jess's boat we found ourselves treading in water.

'The bilge pumps – pump it out,' I ordered, thinking the bilges had just filled up more than usual from the rough crossing.

Jess and the children armed with pots and pans, began bailing out at the same time as Stephen and I operated the pump – but after ten minutes or so, finding the level of water rising rather than falling, we realized the awful truth.

'There must be a hole in the bottom – you must have hit a rock.'

By a stroke of good fortune we were at the quayside of another boat company who also hired boats, and their owner very kindly came to our rescue and between us we managed to pull Jess's boat to a shallow part of the shore, and beach it, half in and half out of the water.

It was then, when we took a look under the bottom, that we had the real shock of our lives – for there was not one but *two* large holes torn in the plywood bottom, as well as a long gash running along the keel. Quite obviously the boat had been badly holed, and was rapidly filling up with water – another mile or two and Jess and Stephen would really have needed their lifebelts!

Suddenly emotionally exhausted, we all sat down in the cockpit of our other boat and looked at one another.

'Phew!'

'That was a narrow squeak!'

Jess folded her arms grimly.

'Well, that's that – we simply can't go back!' She fixed me with a baleful eye. 'And anyway even if you paid me a thousand pounds I wouldn't go across Lough Derg again!'

We were indeed, stranded at Killaloe. Fortunately there was a large hotel attached to the boatyard and for the remaining three days of our holiday we had no alternative but to move in there lock stock and barrel – an expensive but very pleasant sojourn where we experienced the intangible but definite difference of warmth and friendliness between an Irish and English hotel. Meantime the boatyard hauled the boat right out of the water and, after putting off the unhappy moment, I settled down to telephone the bad news to Himself.

Previously we had joked a little between ourselves about the possible reaction. After all it had been a pretty depressing week for Himself, what with the big boat going wrong, and all our other troubles, and his mechanic disappearing for days on end – and now this. Mentally I rehearsed several approaches:

'Do you remember the two motor-boats that set off a week ago. Well …'

'Hullo? This is Mr Baker here. There's been a little bit of trouble …'

'Now don't get worried, but the fact is we hit a rock and …'

In the end Himself took it quite calmly (the boats were after all fully insured). I think he sounded a little taken back when haltingly, at the very end of our conversation I mentioned that we had also lost the dinghy … but as for the rest he told us not to worry and said he would see to getting the boats back.

It was an unexpected ending to our boating holiday. We hired a car for two days and had two memorable trips to Killarney in the south, and up to Galway and Connemara (very like Cornwall) on the north-west coast. At last we were back at Dublin Airport watching the planes, and soon flying twelve thousand feet above and seeing the coastline of Wales below us, and at last the green and red fields of Devon, and sliding down to the firm earth again.

'Well,' said Jess. 'It's hardly been the peaceful relaxing holiday you promised me.'

'No,' I agreed. 'But it's not one you'll easily forget.'

X

Preparing for Portugal

From such tentative boating beginnings as hiring motor cruisers on rivers we had come quite a way by acquiring and learning to handle a 60 foot MFV. Now, nearly twenty years after that momentous day when Jess and I had first come upon our 'seventh child' nestling in a mud berth at Moody's Boatyard, Southampton, we were nearing the end of an ambitious project, spread over several years, of bringing *Sanu* back from the Mediterranean to a more permanent home in Cornwall. This summer we proposed going out to Vilamoura in Portugal, where *Sanu* had spent a quiet winter, and setting off on the 1,500 mile trip, via Portugal, Spain and France, to England.

As is always the case there was to be many a slip before finally we were able to go out to *Sanu*. First, there was the sheer problem of organising the whole affair. Last year, when the boat was berthed at Le Grau-du-Roi in the Camargue district of France I had had to go out before we planned to move and spend three hard weeks working on *Sanu*, along with my friend Bob who came as diesel engineer, and one or two others. On that occasion part of the working time had been occupied in having *Sanu* hauled out of the water and anti-fouling the enormous hull. This year I was not too sure whether we would be able to do this, but at the very worst we could hire skin diving outfits and clean the bottom under the water – the anti-fouling could always be done at leisure once we were back in England, where boatyard charges were not quite on the astronomical level of most of the continental countries.

Because we had done a great deal of work the previous year I hoped that not such a long period would be needed on this occasion, but obviously it would still be necessary for me to go out early with one or two helpers and see to checking the engine, painting the topsides and a few other things of that nature. But who exactly would be coming with me? Here, immediately, were problems. Stephen, once my regular engineer, seemed likely once again to be unable to make the trip, as he and Gina were planning a return visit to her home land of America, along with their two small children, Paris and Amira.

Jess and I were very sad about this, for Stephen has seemed to grow into a permanent part of our life at the Mill House, but we recognised that it was probably important for him to carve out some new direction in his life. Whether he would really be happy in a land with America's standards and values seemed a little doubtful; but then, especially with an American wife eager to get home, perhaps he did not have a great deal of choice in the matter. Either way the hard fact became obvious that with no Stephen I would have to find someone else with an experience of diesel engines. So I wrote off to our friend Bob, who had performed so valiantly last year: fortunately Bob seemed only too happy at the prospect of a repeat performance and what's more there seemed a good prospect of Clive coming, too, another of last year's stalwarts.

Next in my preparations I began gathering some of the thirty or so charts I would be needing. Exasperatingly I knew that most of the charts were in my cabin aboard *Sanu*, as of course I had used them on the original journey out eight years previously; however since I feel it vital to complete all my navigational work well before any journey it seemed worth the extra expense to get a new set of charts – and then, too, they would be more up to date. Once they arrived I followed my usual procedure of devoting every Sunday morning to spreading them out all over my office and carefully mapping out my courses and distances, so that by the time we were due to go I would be totally familiar at least with the navigational aspects of the trip. Often people will suggest that I am being unnecessarily finicky in this sort of approach – surely it could all be left until we are down in Portugal and Spain? Of course that *could* be done, but personally I always feel happier if, like some computer, I have all the relevant information to hand, when required – being left free then to concentrate on more immediate problems, like getting *Sanu* in and out of some minute berth or deciding what to do about that 1,000 foot tanker converging on a collision course!

The strange thing about all this navigational preparation – and I sometimes think members of the family fail to appreciate this point – is that as a result it often seems *to me* as if I have made each trip many months before the actual trip takes place. Certainly there are many Sunday mornings sitting in my little office with charts spread all over the table when I am by no means in Tresidder Valley, near St Buryan, Cornwall – but six or seven hundred miles away aboard *Sanu* perhaps rounding Cape Finisterre or entering Lisbon harbour dominated by its gigantic bridge and huge figure of Christ – or maybe nosing our way into one of those numerous Spanish Rias, like Camarinas, where on our way out from England we had such a marvellous meal in a small worker's taverna.

Of course this year would be rather different to most previous ones. In the past every time I prepared for a *Sanu* cruise I was literally working in unknown territory: we were always embarking to fresh oceans, to new lands and ports. This time we were coming home, and therefore *retracing* our passage, so that most of the ports I was now considering – Lisbon, Leixeos, Vigo, La Coruna, etc, – were places we had already been to before. This makes things much easier, of course, though ten years on there may well have been significant changes in the harbour arrangements. I looked forward now in particular to revisiting Lisbon, one of the most beautiful cities I have ever seen, and also Oporto, that gay Portuguese second capital where the huge vats of the port factories seem almost to line the quays. About Spain I could never feel quite so enthusiastic but since the major part of our cruise looked like taking place in Spanish waters I decided I had better make the best of the bad job. At least later on we

would be back in French waters enjoying the beauties of
Brittany before our final and rather momentous Channel
crossing to Cornwall.

About this time we had a spot of luck, a friend of Stephen's
'Portuguese Tony', who used to live at Gurnard's Head but
had some time ago returned to his native land, appeared in the
district on a fleeting visit intending to pick up a large van he
owned and drive it back to Portugal. When it emerged that in
fact Tony lived at Taira, no more than a few kilometres from
Vilamoura, where *Sanu* lay at rest, and that he would be only
too pleased to carry out for us any equipment we needed for
the boat, Stephen and I quickly drove across at once to
MacSalvers, that marvellous old surplus store near Camborne
whose cavernous interior holds one of the most fascinating
stocks of machinery and equipment I have ever seen. Here I
bought several gallons of anti-fouling and deck paint, also
some canvas for a new awning, and along with an important
item, a spare Calor gas tank, delivered the whole lot one day to
Tony's old van. This certainly was a great relief, for getting
heavy materials out to *Sanu* is always a problem.

Meantime spring had come, summer was almost in the
offing, and life at the Mill House, as ever had taken on an
altogether more pleasant and relaxed air. Already we had
dusted out our garden furniture, put out the swing hammock,
looking forward to those golden days. Of course, before all that
there was – there always is! – some hard work to be done.
Winter floods had left some of the lawn like a quagmire and
we were only now managing to divert the stream and get
things dried out. A new bridge had to be made to Demelza's
caravan – and, speaking of new things, there was the little
matter of our own little porch.

Not often do I allow myself to be committed into such long
term projects, but all through the early spring I was hard at
work making good a boast I had made to Jess: 'Sure, I'll build
you a new porch'.

Six weeks later ... Well, remarkably enough the porch has
been completed and despite unkind criticism from various
members of the family (especially Stephen who went round

saying to his friends, 'That porch at home – *nothing* to do with me – that's Denys's work!' – professional jealousy of course!) – the result had been quite a success. I had indeed thought the matter over quite carefully, and gone to great lengths to give the porch a slate roof and line its walls with granite, so that the whole thing merged in with the ancient appearance of the rest of the house. All the same I *could* have messed things up – whereas in fact, thanks to incorporating two huge windows in which Jess now put some delightful plants, including an amazing two foot high Amaryllis with three lovely rich red petals, the porch interior had become quite an attraction in itself. Though small it was big enough to allow for a seat for three people, where you could sit in hothouse conditions looking out upon the garden and all the flowering trees and shrubs (and also, of course, keeping an eye on the lane and any unforeseen visitors).

Anyway, our visitor at this time was a welcoming one, or rather two – Sydney and Daphne Sheppard, out from Trevail Mill at Zennor. Both of them had been ill lately, and Daphne subjected to a painful operation, so it was good to see them bravely cheerful – and amusing to see standing in the lane Sydney's latest toy, a huge shining old Jaguar of which he was inordinately proud, demonstrating how at the flick of a switch he could make all sorts of things, like windows, operate on their own. (I thought it wisest not to tell Sydney the rather gruesome account I once heard of a man who was strangulated by one such window.)

It was really marvellous to see them both. We gathered not as usual in the house, but over in Demelza's caravan, where somehow in addition to being extremely cosy and intimate, one gets an entirely new perspective on the Mill house, seeing it in all its glory, with the rockeries and trees rising up in the background, and the sound of the gurgling stream almost under Demelza's caravan.

For Demelza, alas, the year 1980 had not been a very good one. At the beginning of the year her flat had been burgled, and the insurance negotiations had been dragging on a long time. Now once again she was involved with insurers and assessors owing to an accident to her car on the Land's End Road. Because the car was a foreign one, surrounded by the mystique that only specialised firms can deal with such rare creatures, Demelza had meekly agreed to the car being towed a long way 'up-country' in Cornwall – a decision she had cause to regret later as she faced delay after delay in getting the work completed. Whereas, as we told her, if she had only had the car taken in to our local garage at St Buryan she would have been able to deal with things on the spot on a personal basis with someone she knew. But there it is ... such situations are enough to drive strong men round the bend, and the effect 'on a somewhat neurotically inclined Demelza was disastrous for us all. For weeks until that damn car was finally mended there was little peace at the Mill House.

For others among our family there were varying fortunes. Taking the good news first Jane had been getting on tremendously at the BBC, her name appearing in the credits every week; for one programme the children's feature 'Grange Hill', she received a BBC internal award. On the other side of the coin, one morning Martin drove up looking thoroughly miserable and announced that he would have to give up his valiant attempts to start up his own printing business and go up to London and get some work there. Apparently there had been a total dearth of business for a whole month and he had come to believe that he simply could not manage to keep solvent ... Having often been through such crises ourselves Jess and I were able to persuade him that if only he could hang on a little longer prospects could change. We were by no means really sure of this, but by a lucky chance the very next week a good order came in, and then another, and suddenly Martin was smiling again.

A third member of the family, Stephen, was smiling too: which meant, as it usually does in his case, that he was happily embarked on yet another of his much enjoyed tasks of demolition and reconstruction – this time on his own little home, the chalet. Rather touchingly to Jess and me, as the time grew nearer for Stephen to embark on his long trip to America, so he seemed subconsciously to be burying himself more and more into the physical reality of his little grey home in the west. Already he had borrowed the rotavator and carved himself out two little lawns around the chalet: he had also managed at last to stop the leaks that had made life so difficult. Now suddenly he had decided to knock a door between his kitchen and the next door living room, so completely altering the atmosphere and making life much easier and more sociable ... and he also built a new table out of our own trees.

Meantime Alan and Gill were down from London, and Alan was plodding away at the setting up of his ambitious wooden studio from where he hoped to produce many masterpieces for the future.

It was Alan, now, who heard of a portable building for sale which might well suit Jess's plans for expanding her smallholding. So began another of the Tresidder epics! This time we had to transport a large portable building by lorry from Redruth to our house. Not such a formidable undertaking? Well, unfortunately the building was in six-foot sections which were heavy and awkward to carry, the lorry that brought them was too big to get down our lane, and so – well let's spare the sheer physical exhaustion of carrying them all down the lane – suffice to say that in the long run the building reached its site. In the meantime we had hired a JCB to level out the ground above Jess's orchard, tearing away all the uncomfortable gorse bushes and leaving a nice flat surface on which to put up the new shed. Quite apart from its gardening aspects the position was superb and we looked forward to being able to bask in the sunshine and enjoy the views which are the reward for a rather exhausting climb to our top field.

In between all this activity yet another strand in the Val Baker tapestry had been entwined a little further. From the time we came to the house Genevieve had had the use of an old caravan up at the north end of the property, but it was a very derelict and leaky old place. Now that she was planning to spend a great deal more time designing and producing her marvellous ceramic plates, with designs from Beardsley and fairy myths and so forth – several of them she had sold in America on a recent visit – well, we all felt it would be not only nice but practical to tear down the old caravan and put up a similar sized wooden hut in its place that was not only weather proof but would be specially designed inside to give Genevieve plenty of space for her work.

At first I was all for ringing up MacSalvers and getting them to tow away the derelict caravan but at the last minute Stephen stepped in, eyes avariciously looking at the aluminium covering of the caravan. Although I protested, he and the others argued persuasively that it would be more profitable for them to dismantle the caravan and take the aluminium off and sell it to the scrap yard. To my chagrin they proved right. Which goes to show something or other.

To compensate myself for this disappointment I concentrated on doing some practical work on Genevieve's new place, levelling out the land and laying a series of concrete blocks as foundations for the portable building. I can never get interested in gardening, much to Jess's despair but I do quite enjoy building huts and the like, and once again I found myself spending happy hours just levelling and building. Soon the site was ready for the hut, and indeed Genevieve's replacement for her caravan was finally ready even before the summerhouse.

Yes, one way and another, family life at the Mill House was very much on the go ... And so, too, very soon, must I be on the go. In no time at all it appeared the summer was really upon us, and it was time to be making those familiar annual arrangements for being on the move again. Sometimes I look back in amazement to think that now for nearly fifteen years I have spent every August out of my own country – a fact I know because sadly I have not been present to celebrate Martin's birthday, on August 7th, since he was still a teenager (correspondingly, Demelza's August 30th birthday has been celebrated almost every one of the past fifteen years at sea aboard *Sanu*!).

There was indeed a time when we used to attempt an Easter cruise in *Sanu* as well as the summer one – I have always

remembered two of these in particular, once a trip through the
Dutch Canals (a little too early alas for the full blooming of
the tulips) and, second, arriving in the heart of Paris in the
middle of an Easter snowstorm! In recent years however our
Mediterranean exploits had involved such intricate planning
and expense that the idea of Easter cruises had had to be
dropped – though once the boat was back in England that
might be something to look forward to.

In the meantime there was a point I had to check up before
leaving – just where was *Sanu* to find her new resting place
back in her home country? It seemed we had two choices,
between Falmouth on the south coast and Hayle on the
north, and I set out to investigate the possibilities of both. As
it happened we had what might be called 'in-depth'
experience of both harbours in those early years when we were
nervously learning to know our boat, keeping her first on a
permanent mooring at Falmouth, later (because it was nearer
our then home at St Ives) against the quay at Hayle. I shall
always remember our first approach to Hayle, a harbour only
accessible by crossing a notorious sand bar which can only be
crossed towards high tide. Even at high tides the channel is a
narrow and difficult one; periodically quite large cargo boats
are stranded at the narrow neck and have to be towed off by
tugs or the local lifeboat. On paper, even in those early days I
was sufficiently confident to feel I was capable of navigating
Sanu into Hayle. But in fact when the time came it was a wild,
wind-blown day and the sea was pretty choppy ...

'Go on,' said Jess, 'Have a pilot the first time. Then you'll
feel safe.'

So we had one of the weather beaten old St Ives pilots and
were very glad of his services, for in fact the sea was quite
heavy and we had the rather uncanny experience of literally
'surfing' into the narrow channel. I would have been petrified
on my own but the pilot appeared quite unruffled, giving a
running commentary as we approached about how we must
fix two beaches in line and steer for them with Lelant Church
just behind. In his wish to be helpful he went out of his way to
tell us when we were just a few feet over the bar, jovially

pointing out swirling white froth which indicated patches where we might easily have gone aground. One way and another there had been some breathless moments before finally we passed over the bar and crept slowly up to our destination, Lelant Quay, near the ferry crossing and golf course.

No sooner had we paid the pilot than he was off in a waiting motor boat to go out to sea and pilot in one of the coal tankers lying around waiting to come into Hayle and unload. In fact this stretch of north coast of Cornwall is so bereft of sheltered harbours that Hayle is quite a busy seaport. Long before we had our own boat Jess and I used to like going down to the beach and watch with fascination from Lelant as quite large ships glided past us, towering high above our puny figures at the water's edge. Of course bringing a 300-ton tanker into Hayle was a considerably trickier job than bringing in a 60-foot MFV. Nevertheless now we felt a sense of real comradeship!

Also there were practical advantages of being at Hayle. At Lelant Quay, and later another quay further in to the town, just below Harvey's, we were able to benefit from the tidal rise and fall, so that for several hours between each tide *Sanu* leaned against the quay and we could work on the hull. Yes, one way and another Hayle would seem to have much to recommend it as the latest home for our wandering baby – always assuming we made it from far away Portugal!

Falmouth, on the other hand, seemed to hold a rather more romantic attraction. When we first acquired our boat we brought her down from Southampton to Falmouth, and there on a permanent mooring right in the middle of the harbour, just off the main town centre, *Sanu* made her home for nearly two years. And what a home: berthed in the centre of what has been described as one of the world's most beautiful natural harbours, a vast circular area of water absolutely studded with boats of all kinds, tugs, fishing boats, yawls, sloops, racing yachts, the Tall Ships – surely there can be few more romantic anchorages in the boating world?

We all looked back most happily on those carefree days

when every weekend we would drive over from St Ives, borrow
a dinghy from the Falmouth Boat Co, our landlords, row out
to *Sanu*, and embark on a busy weekend of titivating our proud
new possession. It was from Falmouth we made our initial
rather hesitant ventures into the unknown waters around the
Cornish coast – from Falmouth we sailed first to Mevagissey –
later to Plymouth, then to Penzance, on to the Scillies – indeed
from Falmouth we set off on most of our early trips, to the
Channel Isles to the Western Isles of Scotland, to Ireland, to
Paris, to Holland and its tulip fields. Yes, Falmouth had a lot
going for it, and the Falmouth Boat Company had already
offered us a permanent mud berth at their dock at Little
Falmouth Boatyard over at Flushing. This would certainly
offer more privacy than Hayle, where *Sanu* would simply lie
alongside the long quay in line with a dozen or more fishing
boats, subject to a lot of coming and going.

Well of course the only thing to do was to go and inspect
whatever sites were available. First Jess and I had a wander
up and down the long quay at Hayle, somewhat daunted by
the enormous drop from the quay, so that at low tide even the
big fishing boats there seemed at the bottom of a pit – we did
not terribly fancy having to climb up and down such heights
every time we wanted to board *Sanu*! Also, there was this great
problem at Hayle of the bar across the entrance, meaning that
one could only leave or arrive at fixed periods. Mmmh! We
drove on to Falmouth, and quickly cleared up the position
there. Despite all their promises it was evident that the
Falmouth yard was pretty tied up, and even if we went there it
would be on a temporary basis.

As it happened, almost at the last minute, we had had a
third offer – to leave the boat at Mylor Harbour Marina. I had
never been there before, but as it was only a mile or two
beyond Flushing we drove over. I was at once impressed not
merely with the beauty of the setting, but with the
practicality: a sheltered little bay full of boats on moorings,
plus a useful line of chandleries, and other boating supplies,
plus the fact that there was a long quay specially for larger
boats such as *Sanu*; *plus* of course the encouraging fact that

Derek Rowe, the manager, remembered *Sanu* well, and seemed delighted at the prospect of her settling at his small and rather cosy marina.

So that in the end was the rather obvious solution. Off to Vilamoura practically in the morning, so to speak – and when finally, we hoped, *Sanu* ended her eight week journey homewards we would simply head for the Lizard and then sail across to Pendennis Castle, Falmouth and the famous Black Rock buoy, and then head up river to Mylor and our new berth there. It would certainly be handy in the future for all sorts of voyages – to the Scillies, to Ireland, to Scotland, some day further afield in the other direction up the river to Paris again, into Holland, and perhaps even over to Norway, a trip we always fancied. Yes, even though we had left the Mediterranean, *Sanu*'s life would not by any means be over!

XI

Sanu Sails Again

After all our preparations it still came as a slight cultural shock to find ourselves one day gliding out of the sky down into the small airport at Faro in Portugal, bound for the marina at Vilamoura.

'Ourselves' on this occasion consisted of Jess and myself and our youngest daughter, Genevieve – the family representatives on this last rather important leg of the three-year saga of bringing *Sanu* home. Awaiting us on the boat was our friend Bob who had looked after the engines on last year's trip around the Balearic Isles: like most who ever entered *Sanu*'s cavernous engine room he had become totally hooked on the beaming old Kelvin, and was determined to nurse it safely back to England.

Equally determined to be in at the finish were two other members of last year's crew, Bob's friend Clive, a woodwork teacher from London, and our old friend from Cornish days, Uni, who was not only a lively raconteur, a cordon bleu cook and a musician, but also a dab hand at carpentry who had already mended several important *Sanu* faults. Clive and Uni were joining us a little way along the Portuguese coast, but Bob had been at Vilamoura for nearly a month already – a fact we soon appreciated, for the boat was looking unusually spick and span, much cleaner than usual. Ah, *Sanu*! How marvellous after all the winter worries to find her nestling demurely at her mooring in a corner of the big marina.

As is always the case with *Sanu*, no sooner had we stepped aboard than it was as if we had stepped back in time. Gone was the green world of the Mill House and Tresidder, replaced in a flash by that old familiar world of water and ropes and moorings and penteens and other boats and throbbing engines and clinking mass. As marinas go, Vilamoura was reasonably attractive, though expensive, and at least it had proved a safe haven. It certainly provided a pleasant enough setting for the next two weeks, during which time the four of us worked hard on the final preparations for what (we hoped not too literally!) was to be the final voyage of *Sanu's* homeward journey. While Bob continued tinkering about with the innards not merely of the Kelvin but also the Lister side engine and the generator, at the same time checking up on submersible pumps and the like, Jess and Genny and I divided our time between painting the decks and the sides of the wheelhouse. Thanks to an earlier delivery of paints by our friend Portuguese Tony we had plenty of materials to hand, and with the sun high and the bustle of everyday marina life all around it was really a pleasure each day to be out on the deck wielding a paint brush.

One of our ever-lasting and ever-unfulfilled aims has been really to weather-proof *Sanu's* decks, to stop the perpetual leaks into the saloon and cabins, and to this end I had been persuaded to buy several huge tins of ex-Admiralty deck paint from MacSalvers. Now while I religiously painted half the bow deck with moderate success Jess, in a misguided effort to make the paint go further, mixed water with a paint intended only to be mixed with turps, with the result that the half she painted continued to leak as badly as before. In short, our deck painting efforts were to prove a waste of time as we discovered to our discomfort during the first Portuguese summer storm. Fortunately some of our other efforts had better results. I spent several days standing in the Zodiac slapping blue and white paint around *Sanu's* ample form, and had the pleasure at the end of seeing what looked almost like a new boat, all polished and gleaming. Meanwhile Genevieve and Jess did some interior painting, turning the cabins back into civilised places.

At last came the great day for leaving Vilamoura. First, we filled up with fuel. Gas oil, rocketing in price all over the world, by some miracle was still relatively cheap in Portugal. In fact in the course of our journey we were to find that Portugal was far the cheapest country in Europe, with the possible exception of Greece, and later in the trip we often looked back lovingly to carefree days where we ate magnificent meals at not much more than £2 a head in pleasant little harbourside bistros.

After the gas oil and water, there came the delicate matter of settling up at the marina office. I had expected a fairly large bill but was presented with an even larger, indeed rather ridiculous one. Fortunately the head of public relations was around and happened to know my name as a writer for English yachting magazines, and I had a shrewd suspicion that perhaps this factor played some part in enabling us to get the bill trimmed to a more realistic figure. Even then it was bad enough, but we could hardly grumble. *Sanu* had survived another winter, and now here she was with her high bow emerging proudly into the open sea again ...

For our first trip I had decided to take up the enticing prospect of anchoring for the night at Sagres, a tiny fishing port nestling at the side of one of Europe's most famous natural headlands, Cape St Vincent, where southbound sea traffic turns left to head for Gibraltar after the long journey across the Bay of Biscay and down the coasts of Spain and Portugal. The Cape itself makes a magnificent if rugged sight, huge cliffs crowned by a very tall and solid lighthouse, and – at least on the picture postcard view I had obtained – Sagres looked a marvellously sheltered little harbour, full of brightly-coloured fishing boats.

Alas, with our usual luck, by the time we reached Sagres the calm weather had changed to a blustering sea, and the wind veered southerly so that it was blowing straight into the otherwise protected harbour. As a result, instead of the romantic peaceful moonlight night I had envisaged, with the four of us eating under our new awning brought out from England, perhaps idly watching the bobbing lights of the fishing boats around us as we sipped our glasses of wine – instead of that we had to anchor in a Force 6 wind, the chain fearfully taut, surrounded by other boats tossing in the wild waves. Conditions were so bad that we had to keep a nervous anchor watch all night, and as things had not improved much in the morning we decided we might as well set off round Cape St Vincent on our next leg to Sines further up the west coast.

Going round Cape St Vincent in a huge swell plus a fierce southerly wind was hardly the most peaceful of experiences, and before long Jess retired to her cabin declaring she would be leaving the boat at Lisbon! Fortunately conditions improved, and when we reached Sines we were delighted to find ourselves anchored in a lovely little bay beneath the tall Moroccan-style buildings of a pleasant little town. The weather had definitely changed for the better, and it was in a flat calm and brilliant sunshine that the next day we completed the first leg of our long journey home, following the flat coast round and easing our way a little nervously across the sand-banked entrance of the River Tagus and into Belem yacht basin in the heart of Lisbon.

From now on for Jess and myself the journey would be a return one, as nearly ten years previously she and I, together with four friends but no other members of the family, had taken the boat out from Fowey round Gibraltar and into the Mediterranean. This meant we were returning to familiar territory: at Lisbon, for instance, we enjoyed showing off to Bob and Genny such delights as the magnificent nautical museums at Belem, and the Gulbenkian Art Gallery, full of original paintings by Rembrandt, Van Gogh, Constable, etc. We also took an ancient tram along the sea-front into Lisbon's Soho, the Alfama, a weird district of clambering hills and twisted buildings, where we were able to enjoy a meal sitting at tables out on the pavement. On another night we sampled one of the main delights of Portuguese social life, visiting one of the special cafés where to the accompaniment of a bottle of *Vino verde* you could sit for hours listening to the Portuguese 'Fado' singers, travelling musicians who visit one café after another with their guitars, singing the haunting folk songs of the district.

After spending four days in Lisbon we were greatly relieved

to emerge on deck and see a familiar figure squatting on the quayside. After a mammoth journey from London to Plymouth and via the 24-hour ferry to Santander, a lift to Madrid and a train down to Lisbon – Uni had arrived. At once his cheerful presence raised our spirits enormously, and we began to look forward any moment to the arrival of our fifth member, Clive, though it had been agreed that if he didn't appear at Lisbon by the allotted time for departure we should carry on and expect him to find us at one of the next points on the itinerary.

And so he did, though not quite according to plan! First we called in at one of the most delightful places of the trip, a real old-fashioned fishing port, Peniche, opposite the Isles of Berlenga. Peniche was dominated by rows of big steel Portuguese fishing boats, mostly about 90 feet long: we tied up alongside one of these, which meant having to get up at six in the morning to help them to set off for their day's fishing, but it was well worth it, for the men were cheerful and friendly and the port itself of great interest, with dozens of sardine bars and little clusters of people with charcoal fires cooking their evening meal on the pavement.

In fact Peniche was full of colour and atmosphere, and the only thing lacking when we left was our friend Clive. Ah well, we said, he'll be waiting for us at Figueira da Foz. So he was, did we but know it, but while he waited at a quay up the river, we had decided to anchor for the night just outside, and by some unlucky chance he never actually saw *Sanu*'s familiar shape. So the next morning, after a very uncomfortable night in the Atlantic swell, we upped anchor at dawn and went on our way to Leixeos ... where in due course, slightly disgruntled but relieved to be with us, Clive appeared at the quayside.

Leixeos was our last port in Portugal, and we anticipated merely two days there – in the event we were trapped there ten days, owing to worn bearings in the main engine. Fortunately by now Bob had Clive to help him: between them they took the entire engine to pieces two or three times – at any rate, whatever measures they took finally proved successful, thank goodness. In between we had a series of interesting expeditions. On one we had a marvellous cheap meal in a little backstreet restaurant: on another we took a bus into the real centre for that area, Portugal's second biggest city, Oporto. Jess and I had memories of a previous visit where we all went round the headquarters of Sandeman's, the big port firm – so it was with great expectations that we set off on a Saturday afternoon across the ancient bridge, only to find Sandeman's closed. Moreover, most of the other port depots seemed equally forbidding and closed.

Just as we were losing heart we were directed by a friendly local up and up a winding hill and finally reached the huge headquarters of Warre and Co., one of the oldest of all the port makers, there to find everything open and in full swing. After a rather perfunctory glance at the vats (Warre's claimed to have the largest single vat in the whole world, and it certainly looked like it) we settled down at wooden tables and were plied with half a dozen different vintages of port. By the time we finally emerged into broad daylight again it was all we could do to make our sleepy way back to the boat.

It was at Leixeos that we met the local Mr Fixit, a suave refugee from Angola who had set himself up as a ship's agent and soon talked me into such a bemused state that I found myself ordering so-called duty free cases of Vino Verde, Mateus Rose, Carlsburg beer and a few other important alcoholic items. Later of course I discovered many of these could be bought for the same price in the local shops, but at least it saved a lot of bother to have the whole lot delivered in one go – even if it did mean a rather consistent diet of Portuguese wine for the rest of the trip.

When finally we left Leixeos, and Uni had climbed up on top of the wheelhouse and taken down our Portuguese courtesy flag, substituting the red and yellow Spanish one, somehow there was a lifting of spirits. It was not that we had not liked Portugal; indeed we preferred the Portuguese people to the Spanish, but the fact was that weatherwise Portugal had been very disappointing. Now we hoped that Spain would bring a change of tone. At our first port of call, Bayonna, we immediately felt that this was coming to pass, for after a rather breathtaking entrance between heaps of outer reefs and rocks – which, we were to learn, are a familiar part of Spanish nautical geography – we found ourselves anchored in a most beautiful spot, with mountains rearing all around, and little cafés lining the harbour. That evening we sat at the back of the boat watching the dying sunshine, surrounded by other yachts peacefully at anchor, drinking our wine and eating a marvellous meal made by Uni, and the world seemed a pleasant place indeed. There was even swimming off the side of the boat, a pastime that had been a daily feature of life in the Mediterranean, but singularly lacking so far on this trip.

The next day on to Camarinas, one of the really nostalgic ports for Jess and myself. We had never forgotten an unexpected five course meal in a delightful old world Spanish restaurant – and now, of course, we insisted on trying to repeat the experience, only to find that we simply could not find the restaurant at all! Just as we stood around feeling deflated we were caught up by some French yachtsmen full of bonhomie who assured us they knew a really good fish restaurant and guided us up a winding back alley until, sure enough, we found ourselves installed in a place not unlike the one Jess and I remembered. It wasn't the same place, of course, but the experience was just as good in its way.

When we got back to *Sanu* we found the Frenchmen, occupying between them two large yachts, and anchored close by, calling out, 'If we bring a bottle of whisky can we join you and play some music?' They had, of course, noticed our resident musicians, Genny and Uni, with their saxophone and violin: now they all came aboard, no fewer than fifteen of them, including a couple of guitarists, and in no time we found ourselves in the middle of one of those marvellous and unexpected *Sanu* evenings, singing familiar songs, chattering away and imbibing a mixture of French, Portuguese and Spanish wine, and whisky! As ever we were fascinated at the numbers carried by these comparatively small French yachts, eight on one, seven on another. We were impressed to learn that they had just sailed right across the Bay of Biscay, and after only a week down the coast proposed turning round and being back in France at the end of ten days. They were certainly tough seamen, those French.

After the comparative tranquillity and quiet of Camarinas, a small fishing port, the next day we headed for the famous 'Hercules', the world's only functioning lighthouse from classical antiquity – and the large city of La Coruna, which marks the very tip of north-western Spain. Our previous visit to La Coruna had marked the welcome end of a 48-hour crossing of the Bay of Biscay, but all the same Jess and I had not been greatly impressed. This time we were much more attracted and found it to be a really smart and sophisticated city, full of good shops and cafés, and bustling with life.

It was also the place where the remainder of our crew joined us in the form of an Australian girl, Lyn, who had been on *Sanu* on our Italian trip two years before, together with her boy friend, Tim, and another friend, Judith, neither of whom had experienced *Sanu* travel before. It was good to see fresh faces, as it all adds to the enjoyment of the voyage, and also spreads out the cooking chores. Now we only had to cook once every nine days! Here let me say hastily and with my hand on my heart that though styles could be said to have varied, everyone made great efforts when it was their cooking night, and memories are of many mouth-watering meals. Perhaps outstanding among these I think was one done by Uni where he cooked the whole meal on deck using a Portuguese pottery open brazier.

Leaving La Coruna turned another corner, as I had decided that instead of crossing the Bay of Biscay direct, as we had done on the outward trip, we would follow the coast of Northern Spain as far as Santander before crossing to La Rochelle. Now for us began what was initially a delightful period of voyages up tiny picturesque Spanish *rias*, where we got involved in an incredible series of fiestas – then subsequently a time of considerable nautical trauma. To take the more tranquil memory first, there were idyllic stays at picturesque little fishing ports like Cedeira, Vivero and Ribadeo – marred only by a misbegotten decision to 'eat out' at Vivero where the entire party were ripped off by a Spanish fish bar which actually had the nerve to charge 200 pesetas (about £1.30) for rolls of bread.

When travelling abroad nothing is more pleasant or interesting than eating out in local restaurants and in the past we have done our fair share – indeed it was almost a custom to have at least one meal out at each port where we stayed any length of time. This year we were feeling the financial squeeze, and apart from two or three special occasions evening meals were confined to aboard.

Fortunately this was no great hardship as it seems there is nothing like a certain sense of competition for bringing out the cordon bleu element that seems to lurk somewhere in everyone. Certainly I found a source of constant amazement in the meticulous manner each cook went about his or her daily task. Some, like myself, tended to rely heavily on old established and oft rehearsed dishes, in my own case cheese pie or macaroni, and admittedly this showed no great sweep of imagination. Others, like Uni and Genevieve and Jess, were often inspired to great dishes. I think we would all agree that Uni showed the most masterly touch, invariably producing not merely a two-course but a three-course dinner – what was more exasperating for us other poor cooks, especially the one due to follow next day, he could even turn out something very special for lunch. For most of us this was regarded as a scratch meal, something simple like bread and cheese and fruit, but Uni would serve up some immaculate spread of salad, omelette aux herbes, baked potatoes, etc.

He was certainly a difficult cook to follow, but Jess and Genny made several impressive efforts, and I shall always remember with wry affection Genny's grimly determined effort to serve a really high-class meal, including several individually cooked dishes, on our very last voyage crossing the English Channel in the middle of a Force 8 gale!

Cedeira, Vivero, Ribadeo: the names reel pleasantly off the tongue and that was their place in our itinerary, lovely settings, a sense of relaxation and enjoyment. However the best was yet to come – just as the worst was to follow that.

From Ribadeo we sailed on to a little fishing port called
Luarca. When I say 'little', the chart indicated a small
harbour and we expected to be somewhat confined ... and
indeed on first arrival we were quite alarmed to find seemingly
just a very small circular basin and no more. We tied up by a
barren-looking quay realising uneasily that when the tide
went out we might well be aground; then looking around
desperately we caught the attention of a local fisherman who
made an expressive gesture to one corner and indicated quite
clearly that we needn't be worried. Following his directions
we nosed our way into a small channel which led leisurely
round a bend and then, hey presto, all at once we found
ourselves in quite a large inner basin absolutely packed with
large fishing boats and yachts. It was all rather alarming with
a big boat like *Sanu* having to manoeuvre around on the
proverbial sixpence, but we managed to tie up alongside a big
Spanish fishing boat whose captain seemed not to mind,
indeed obviously rather welcomed the company of a boatload
that included several attractive young ladies in bikinis.

Thus began the saga of Luarca, one of the real high spots of
Sanu's voyage that summer. From the moment we set foot on
land we had the feeling that we had hit upon an unusual
place, and this was certainly so. In the guide book Luarca is
described as 'one of the most beautiful cities on the Asturaian
coast' and this was no exaggeration, for someone with
imagination had emphasised all the natural attractions. For
instance, the River Negro winds through the city as a
backbone, and all the way along the quays the local
authorities had fixed coloured flower pots in large barrels, so
that there was an immediate feeling of gaiety. Gaiety, indeed,
is the word we shall always associate with Luarca, though this
was perhaps encouraged by the fact that, unknown to us, we
had picked just about the best three days in the year in which
to arrive there, for starting the next day Luarca was about to
celebrate one of Spain's great annual events, the Feast of
Ascension (what is sometimes called 'The Great Week').
Initially the festival has religious connections but beyond that
it spills over into a feast of entertainment and this was the side

we now got caught up in. Beginning, for us, with the night of the high wire act.

What happened was that on the first afternoon when Jess and I went out for a stroll we came upon the city square and were intrigued to find it quite dominated by an incredible high wire that began down in one corner of the square and stretched, taut and quivering, for a distance of several hundreds of feet right up to the top of a huge office block which was at least twenty storeys high. Furthermore, at the foot of the wire there stood, fixed on a steel platform, a high speed motor bike (the sort used in speedways), the hard rubber wheels of the bike having been carefully indented down the middle so that they fitted on to the wire. Obviously something rather special was planned for that evening and we decided this must not be missed.

Lyn was the cook for that night so it was arranged that she should get the meal ready, then leave it to warm in the oven. After all, no doubt the high wire act whatever it was would be over in half an hour or so. We should have known! At eight o'clock the entire population of Luarca appeared to have gathered in the sizeable square with us among them. It was a real fiesta occasion, whole families in groups, grannies and children as well as young and middle-aged – a truly festive air. Every now and then a loudspeaker would blare out the announcements, presumably of the imminence of the performance. Of course we had all assumed that there would simply be a single startling ride of a motor cycle up the trapeze wire, but this in fact was merely to be the finale.

After several announcements, interposed with some excruciatingly loud interval music (the main tune, of all things, being 'Amazing Grace') suddenly there appeared the figure of a young man adorned in a crimson suit with white frills which made a striking background to his own dark skin and curly black hair. (Later we discovered he was Moroccan.) This was Peppi, one of a group of trapeze artistes called the Bordinos who, though we had no idea at the time, are famous all over Europe and further afield (even as I write they are amazing audiences over in South America). Before our impressed gaze Peppi casually picked up a long balancing pole and after rubbing his feet once or twice in resin, calmly and confidently set out to walk up the steeply inclined trapeze wire from the ground level at one end of the square to the top of the office building. Not only did he accomplish this journey safely but he gave us several heart attacks on the way by calmly pausing, balancing on one leg and holding the other in mid-air. It was a most impressive performance that drew loud applause; but there was more to come. Even as Peppi stood on top of the office building taking his bow there came a hum from the crowd and we suddenly realised that a second wire walker had set off from the bottom.

This time it was Daniel, a young boy (actually sixteen we discovered) wearing a blue silk costume, and with a crop of blond hair. He too went through much the same motions as Peppi, but with the difference that he paused halfway up the line and waited while Peppi slowly came back down the line. The two of them then sat down, as if perfectly at ease, legs dangling casually either side of the line. Now a third figure appeared setting out to climb the line, this time the head of the group, Manuel, and he was tight-rope walking blindfolded. As he walked on, keeping a very slow pace, gingerly putting one foot before the other, you could have heard a pin drop among the crowd, for one of the impressive things about these performances was that they were carried out from beginning to end without any sort of safety net. At last Manuel came up to the boy in blue, felt with his toe, lifted his feet, very carefully stepped over him and carried on walking! Next he did the same with Peppi, then, just to complete an astounding performance, went on and on until he stepped triumphantly upon the top of the office building.

Naturally the crowd hooted and cheered like anything, ourselves among them, but things were by no means finished. While we stared in fascination at the tiny figures outlined against the sky by the office rooftop, I remarked anxiously, 'Look at that blindfold man, if he's not careful he'll be falling over.'

I stopped speaking then, aghast, for that was exactly what

seemed to have happened – but fortunately not quite. What really took place was that while we had been watching, rather puzzled, Manuel had manoeuvred himself into a position where he could clasp a ring in his teeth, this ring being hooked round the wire ... now like a bolt from the blue he came flashing down the wire at high speed his body dangling in mid air, held on only by this teeth! As he sped towards the ground there was a great 'Oooh', but wisely he had taken the precaution beforehand to have several ropes attached to the wire near the ground end, these being held by trusted companions who by pulling on the ropes at the right moment slowed down the final arrival to bearable pace.

'Bravo! Bravo!' shouted the crowd, or I suppose, 'Ole! Ole!'

They were still in the middle of shouting their approval when there was another loud gasp as a second figure came hurtling down. This time it was the boy in blue not hanging on by his teeth, but tied on by his ankle and hanging face downwards! He, too, travelled like a bullet but was slowed up at the last moment.

Finally, if I remember right, for by now we were totally confused by the proliferation of stupendous performances, I think Peppi then came down with one of the others hanging from a frame below the wire.

At long last, the finale. This time it was Manuel, the leader of the troupe, who appeared dressed flamboyantly as a motorcyclist, complete with silver helmet. He mounted the bike and revved up the engine but instead of shooting up like a bullet with flames coming from the exhaust as I had imagined, he actually drove up the wire at quite leisurely pace – so leisurely in fact that halfway up he had the temerity to stop the bike and sit there motionless, balanced perfectly. Hardly had our cheers risen up than he *reversed* the bike back to the ground! As if that was not enough he roared up again, steadied the bike, and proceeded to carry out a series of acrobatic exercises, ending up standing on his hands on the saddle of the bike half way up the wire, balanced some two hundred feet above the square.

I can truthfully say it was one of the most memorable

experiences of any *Sanu* trip and though little to do with boats perhaps we were geared up to appreciate the bravery of the men because risk is what going to sea is all about, though of course there is little comparison between sitting on a fat but safe old boat and balancing on a trembling wire. As the conclusion of the act Manuel took the motor bike right up to the office roof and then reversed full speed down with the other two wire-walkers dangling from a frame hanging beneath the bike!

By the time we got back to the boat Lyn's supper was somewhat over-cooked but I don't think any of us complained! The truth was we were all rather fascinated by the Bordinos, especially as we discovered that their vans were parked only a few yards from *Sanu*'s berth and in no time Genny and Judith and the others had struck up a great rapport with the artistes. This all came to a social head on the night of the fiesta itself when apparently nobody in Luarca goes to bed. About five in the morning Jess and I heard the rather marvellous sound of Genny playing the saxophone and Uni his violin and, peering blearily out into the dawn, saw the two of them leading a great crowd of singing Spaniards through the streets of Luarca. Truly a night to remember!

All these celebrations continued throughout the great day, crowds singing and the wine flowing, then there was a repeat performance of the wire act in the square followed by further musical gatherings in the bars. This time Jess and I retired exhausted. Early the next morning we found a rather sheepish Genny and Judith (who had been out celebrating all night) asking if it wasn't time the boat sailed. We were rather puzzled at this insistence from two of our usually late risers ... it was only later on, when regretfully we had left Luarca and were out on the high seas, that we learnt the whole complicated story.

The previous evening both girls had got very happily involved with the Bordinos and in the middle of the fiesta celebrations, no doubt affected by the wine, had allowed themselves to be inveigled into promising that the next evening they would both appear as novice wire walkers in the town square! It was quite a serious proposition, as apparently the Bordinos regularly invited people to 'have a go'. However what seemed wildly romantic and exciting at two or three in the morning – well, in the grey dawn of a new day was positively frightening. No wonder Genny and Judith couldn't relax until we were at sea, though of course they did feel duly penitent at breaking a promise. Ah well, sometime in the future I am sure their path and that of the Bordinos will cross again!

XII

Our Spanish Saga

Llanes ... has 28 beaches, all of them with fine yellow sand
bathed by the lively waters of the Cantabrian which, with
the rise and fall of the tides twice a day, keeps them smooth
and even. They are easy of access with nearby green
meadows and urban communication. The district is a
continual festival. In all the pilgrimages, which on Sundays
and holidays are widespread throughout the region, the
main attraction is always the procession and the
performance by young people wearing the typical costume
of the region and dancing the typical *pericotes*, handed down
in all its purity from fathers to sons. From Llanes one goes
through the marvellous settings of the foothills of the Picos
de Europe ...'

Who could have imagined that such an idyllic word picture
would be the smoke screen for *Sanu*'s most terrifying ordeal
since a decade earlier our dear old boat struck a submerged
concrete pillar and sank at Bilbao? I suppose it could be said
that after leaving Rhodes two years previously and then
travelling hundreds of miles, indeed more than 2,000 in all,
along the Pelopennese and down the Messina Straits, round
Stromboli's volcanic island and up the volatile Italian coast
and then hugging the mistral-swept shores of southern France,
after venturing out to the Balearic Isles of Majorca and
Minorca and Ibiza and then following the Spanish coast until
Gibraltar before striking out into the broad Atlantic all the
way round Portugal and western Spain and then heading
eastwards, after accomplishing all that and suffering nothing

much worse than the occasional rough days, after all that, it could be argued, *Sanu*'s crew had perhaps grown a little careless?

Not a bit of it. Let me put the matter into perspective. After our three wonderful days at Luarca we headed along the coast towards a port that on paper was called Gijon but by voice pronounced, it seemed, 'Hee-Haw'. Either way after Luarca it seemed a most dismal and depressing place and we merely spent a necessary night there before moving on.

Next on the itinerary was Santander, our final Spanish port before striking out across the Bay of Biscay for La Rochelle. However Santander was nearly 100 miles away and judging from the relaxed mood of my crew the preference was undoubtedly for daily trips that did not exceed 40 or 50 miles at most. After all there was certainly no point in turning a leisurely cruise into a chore and obviously it made sense to break up the Santander trip with a night at some port half way along the route. After studying our general chart carefully it became apparent that really the only place so positioned was 'the small fishing port of Llanes, population 15,000'. Unfortunately, though I had taken good care to ensure that I possessed a large scale chart of every port we were due to visit on our cruise, Llanes had not figured on this itinerary and so we had no chart for the harbour.

In this matter of charts, by the way, I am always extremely cautious and I had never before taken *Sanu* into any port without the help of either a published chart or at the very least a detailed sketch drawn for me by a fellow yachtsman with experience of the place in question. So now, once we had decided to call at Llanes, I made every effort to find out all the information possible. I read up the *Admiralty Pilot* for the Bay of Biscay and found half a page devoted to the subject of Llanes, explaining that the entrance was not much more than a cable in width (about 500 feet). Boats with a draft of up to 13 feet could make use of the port but, it was emphasised, entrance was best not attempted without local knowledge. As it happens *Admiralty Pilots* are notorious among yachtsmen for their doomladen attitude to almost everything, from wind to fog, from the state of the sea to the size of harbours, and the line 'entrance should not be attempted without local knowledge' is as common as to be rather taken for granted ... and indeed we have entered a large number of such harbours without benefit of local assistance, the fact being that provided one has a detailed chart and applies commonsense there should be no great problem.

Unfortunately on this occasion we had no chart, detailed or otherwise, and a paucity of information, and not surprisingly I was worried. I can remember while at Gijon I went over to some of the local fishermen and questioned them anxiously about Llanes. Sadly none of them spoke English while my Spanish was on the same level and though we managed to make some communication in a sort of bastard French it was really very difficult. One of the fishermen was most helpful and squatted on the pavement and with a piece of chalk actually drew me a sketch of Llanes, and from what he appeared to say all seemed to be well. Just then along came another fisherman, no doubt an older and wiser man, who shook his head dubiously.

From what they said I gathered the impression, more or less correctly as it happened, that indeed we *could* go into Llanes but that at low tide our boat would have to lean against the quay, keel on the ground. This did not worry me unduly as *Sanu* is designed for that sort of thing and indeed once we reached Brittany we expected to be berthing regularly at such drying-out ports. When we got to Llanes all we need do was go up to the quay and immediately put out one of our large wooden supporting legs, and all would be well.

It was important, of course, to enter Llanes around high tide. At such a time, according to the tide tables in *Reed's Almanac*, there would be about 15 feet of water, more than enough to enable *Sanu*'s $7\frac{1}{2}$ foot draft to enter the port and reach a quay. Yes, it sounded OK. Indeed, as we finally set off from Gijon that morning I was far more worried about the business of the harbour entrance width than depths. All the same I was a little disturbed, as time went on, to notice deep down somewhere in the remote recesses of what might be called my innermost being, an unusual sense of unease – what can only be called a 'bad vibe'. The reason I noticed was that I have only had such a feeling twice before in my boating life, and those two unforgettable occasions were at Tresco, on the Isles of Scilly, and at Bilbao, North Spain – the two times in her career, at least in our ownership, when *Sanu* has actually sunk. How I wish I had had the courage to follow my vibes!

Well, I didn't. Instead we sailed on and on along a rather level coastline, dogged at first by a thick mist which gradually cleared into bright sunshine. It was not a comfortable journey as there was a westerly sea striking on our port side so that the boat rocked a good deal. I can remember how after preparing a lunch of shrimps and salad poor Jess had to ask me to serve it while she retired *hors de combat* to her cabin.

In fact soon after lunch the weather worsened and the nearer we came to our planned destination the greater grew my unease. Looking at the nearby coastline I saw waves breaking on the rocks and realised that judging by all the detail I had gathered Llanes harbour would be wide open to such a sea, which meant the entry might not be the simple matter I had hoped would be the case. Even then, though, it was still width that bothered me rather than depth. At one stage I remember calling Uni over and pointing to a small island we were passing and reading out from the *Pilot* the significant detail that the island was separated from the mainland by a channel 'about a cable wide'.

'That's how wide the entrance to Llanes is,' I said.

'Mmmmmh,' said Uni thoughtfully.

'Doesn't look very wide does it?' I said, even more thoughtfully.

Soon we began looking for landmarks, pinpointing our destination about a mile ahead. Yes, there was the outline of houses, there was the Antonio lighthouse. Yes, that was Llanes all right ...

Our spirits fell a little – *chilled* I think would be the right word. The sea was breaking quite heavily on a narrow breakwater that came out from the land. That was bad enough: worse was to come.

'Do you see what I see?' I said.

Yes, they could. Not only was the sea breaking on the outside of the breakwater – but beyond, on the other side, we could quite clearly see waves breaking on the *inside* of the other breakwater! In other words, the sea was as rough inside the harbour entrance as it was outside.

'Well,' I said uneasily. 'Here we go! Looks like a tricky entrance.'

That, as it happened, could be described as one of the understatements of the year, certainly of that year's trip. Even at that late moment perhaps it might have been possible to decide not to enter Llanes and no doubt wiser and more experienced seamen might have chosen such a course. But – well, we had come 50 miles, it was getting rougher, we were all rather tired, and, most important of all, there was literally no other port for miles and miles; indeed it might have been necessary to carry on a further 50 miles to Santander. Whereas here, well once we got in there was the prospect of a safe little haven, we could tie up, put out our leg and relax ...

So we carried out a broad sweeping movement until *Sanu*'s bow faced the entrance to Llanes and at last, not I must admit without a heavy heart and an increasing sense of trepidation, I headed our boat and its motley crew harbourwards.

'It's rather like Hayle, isn't it?' someone said, and we nodded as we remembered the bar at Hayle and the way we often had to surf across it when the weather was rough. Well, the weather was rough here today and Llanes had a sand bar and, yes, we were going to have to surf across it. But then there was a 15 foot tide – surely we would be all right?

'Genevieve,' I said quietly. 'Would you read the echo sounder for me?'

With Genny reading out the depths at regular intervals we started to make our entry. Conditions were certainly what might be called lively. Great lines of breakers poured down the main channel, breaking on either side, and as soon as we had come between the outer harbour arms we were inexorably lifted up and carried along in that familiar surfing motion. Since there were savage looking rocks on either side I had to keep my wits about me to keep *Sanu*'s bow heading in the right direction. But then I had done the same sort of thing on past occasions, not only at Hayle but on entering Audierne in Brittany and the River Herault at Agde, where we used to keep *Sanu* in the winters. It was difficult, indeed, but not impossible; just a touch of the wheel here, another there. Yes, it was going to be all right, we were managing quite nicely – now ahead of us we could glimpse the opening to the inner harbour.

'Twenty feet,' said Genny. Then her voice seemed to change note. 'Sixteen feet – fifteen feet – fourteen, thirteen, twelve – *ten feet*! Hey, Denys, are you quite sure ...?'

We were, alas, committed, there could be no turning back in such a maelstrom.

'*Nine feet*!' said Genny in a high pitched, worried voice. 'Denys, it's only nine feet ...'

It must have been at that moment when we experienced the first dreaded thump as *Sanu*'s iron keel hit ground. Fortunately for us it turned out to be sand, not rock – a slight bonus I suppose you could say.

Thump – thump – it happened again and again, and then again. And then, with a great shudder, the boat ceased moving.

'We're aground!' someone shouted, rather obviously.

We most certainly were, well and truly aground, right in the middle of the outer entrance to Llanes harbour, at about four o'clock on a Sunday afternoon with crowds of sightseers out for their afternoon stroll and now watching with interest this unexpected entertainment. From behind us the great waves came rolling along, sweeping the length of our fat hull and then crashing forward ... Only the fact that we were embedded in sand saved us from slewing sideways – meantime we could see on all sides the granite edges of fearsome rocks.

With no chart to go by we had no idea in which direction we should try and move even if it were possible. We had been aground in our times once or twice before and we knew that by putting a rope to the shore we might just manage to winch ourselves to one side, racing both engines at the same time. But which way?

While we were all debating frenziedly these possibilities a lifeline was literally thrown into our midst. It took the form of the arrival of a motor boat out of which leaped a small swarthy figure who despite his minute size conveyed an immediate air of authority. This was gathered was Llanes' unofficial pilot, who boasted the marvellous name (as we learned later) of Modesto Garcia. I don't suppose any of us are ever likely to forget that moment when this endearing little Spaniard stepped into *Sanu*'s wheelhouse, gave a confident grin, raised a soothing hand, and said:

'Tranquil! Tranquil!'

There followed a stream of Spanish which I took to mean, don't worry, everything will be all right – and then Modesto beckoned me to let him take the wheel, while I operated the engines, obeying his rapid instructions, first to reverse, then to go forward, then reverse, and so on and so forth. A momentary distraction came when a white-faced Bob appeared to announce that the Kelvin engine's water pump had broken down so that it was rather unwise to continue running it much longer. At such a moment in time however only an actual explosion would have persuaded me to shut off the engine, and unhappily Bob agreed we should just have to risk continuing to use it for a little while longer.

Meanwhile our pilot had been busy organising his friend in the motor boat to take our strongest rope ashore and have it tied to a distant bollard at the entrance to the inner harbour. With the other end of this rope wound round our winch several of the crew now began the laborious task of trying to pull the bow round towards the harbour entrance. Every now and then, at Modesto's bidding, I would give a burst on the engines. More ropes, more winching, more bursts of engine power ... it all seemed a hopeless endeavour, but the fact was that in a series of heart-stopping jerks (intermingled with regular bumps on the bottom) *Sanu* actually did move. Only a few feet at a time, true, yet somehow – miraculously almost, since the tide was falling – Modesto managed to get our bow off the original sandbank and facing the harbour entrance.

By now of course half the population of Llanes had gathered

to watch what must have been the spectacle of the year so far as they were concerned. It seemed to us, in our state of general agitation, that some of them might well have contributed more positively than merely shouting conflicting instructions to the unfortunate Modesto who, as obviously his strategy, though correct, was beginning to fail, himself became quite edgy. (Later we learned most of the watchers were tourists out for the day, and that locals would not have been so unsympathetic.)

Every now and then I would look at Modesto inquiringly – each time he would nod re-assuringly, but I must admit I was beginning to have doubts. In the end Modesto actually managed to get *Sanu*'s bow and about one-third of her length into the narrow entrance of the inner harbour ... and there we were well and truly stuck, in a very odd position, but tied up in all directions and at least *safe*.

All this must have taken at least two hours, two of the most traumatic hours of our lives, I imagine. However if we thought we had gained some sort of respite we were quickly disillusioned. One of the inevitable results of the keel pounding on the sands – and thank goodness it was a sandy bottom, for with rocks there would have been little *Sanu* left – was that the hull had been painfully disturbed and at least half a dozen sizeable leaks had developed, with the result that sea water was now literally pouring in. With the Kelvin out of action our usually powerful bilge pumps were inoperable, and for the past hour or so Bob had been desperately juggling about with no fewer than five electric submersible pumps. Alas, one by one they burned out and gave up under the strain and at last we were down to one totally inadequate hand pump. There was nothing for it but the familiar call:

'*Buckets*! Quick now, all the buckets on the boat, down in the aft.'

By now Modesto had departed for a well-earned rest, after promising us he would be back at four in the morning, high tide, when we would pull *Sanu* further up the quay. Most of the sightseers had drifted away, too, as it was already dark and we were left to our own resources – which now became intensely concentrated on the single task of emptying water out of *Sanu* more quickly than it was entering.

In fact the good old-fashioned plastic bucket method is one of the most efficient ways of handling large quantities of water (faster than most forms of pumping) always provided you have sufficient people to handle the operation. Well by good fortune there were nine of us aboard – although of course, while some were seasoned sailors, our three latest recruits, Lyn, Tim and Judith, were new to such an alarming experience. It says much for their good humour and spirit that three hours later they were still slogging away as part of the human chain gang we formed.

What we did was concentrate our energies in the aft cabin, since that was where most water in the bilges ended up. The system was to have one person filling a bucket down in the bilge, pass it to a second standing at the foot of the cabin stairs, who then passed it up to someone standing at the top of the stairs, who then gave it to someone else on deck, who quickly emptied it over the side and then just as quickly passed the bucket across to yet another person standing by the aft cabin reef who then dropped it straight down to the slave in the bilges, who then began the whole process all over again. Although it may sound rather torturous it not only worked but we managed to raise our rate quite remarkably, and at one stage were emptying three buckets a minute. Naturally there were times when individuals became temporarily exhausted but no one had to issue any orders, someone just instinctively took over and gave the tired one a respite. I was proud of my scratch *Sanu* crew that traumatic night in Llanes.

I don't suppose any of us will forget those four or five hours, the regular swinging movements of the red and blue plastic buckets, the smell of diesel, the swinging lights, the occasional miraculous appearance of 'tea and bickies' from the forward bowels of the boat – above all the way voices were cheerfully raised in song so that what might have been a truly depressing experience was somehow transformed into something shared, and therefore more bearable. Danger is a marvellous uniting force, and all minor disagreements and dislikes that may have arisen during the voyage were swept away that night – never to reappear, I might add. When at last, after Modesto had joined us at four o'clock and we had dully pulled *Sanu* along thus freeing the entrance to the inner harbour (we did not realise it then but our accident had grounded the fishing fleet of Llanes for the night!), the tide had fallen sufficiently for the incoming water to stop and we were able to flop down and relax. Well, several of us fell asleep there and then where we sat.

The tide was out for six hours so that we were able to get some sort of rest but of course our dreams were haunted by the knowledge that soon the dreaded water would be creeping up again, and sure enough back it all came – and back we had to go on the buckets. However this time we were heartened by the knowledge that once the tide had gone again it would be the middle of the day and there would at last be a chance to undertake some sort of repairs to the exterior of *Sanu*'s hull. Originally the idea was that Uni and Clive and Bob would do the work and they had already hurried into the town and bought large quantities of mastic and putty and other materials.

However just after they had climbed down the ladder to the beach and were about to begin work there arrived a very determined and formidable Spaniard who was, we gathered, the local shipwright. Seemingly impervious to our feeble protests (for we were naturally worried about incurring possibly huge financial costs) this gentleman opened his toolbag and calmly set to work to mend our leaks. At first Uni, our official carpenter, felt rather put out but as we watched the expert at work, measuring leaks, fashioning long strips of wood to hammer home, caulking with infinite care – suddenly we realised we were in the presence of a real professional and that we would just have to take the risk and leave matters in these capable hands. The others helped where they could, of course, and the next day after our new friend had disappeared on his other job of fishing, completed some extra repairs.

The net result of all this activity, thank goodness, was that gradually *Sanu*'s excessive leaks were reduced from a positive torrent to a mere trickle, something that could easily be coped with by our resurrected submersible pumps. We also once more had the services of the Kelvin, whose water pump problem had been cured by Bob and Clive, and really it was only necessary now to run this for half an hour once a day.

And of course our stay at Llanes was to be one of several days. During this time gradually it occurred to us that we were quite a tourist feature. We failed to understand quite why our misfortunes should be of such great interest – until one of the fishermen told us that in fact we were the biggest boat ever actually to enter Llanes. It was true that boats up to thirteen feet draft *could* enter but previously none had bothered to make the attempt. Fortunately we had come in on a neap tide which meant that for the rest of the week the tides would be a little higher each day so we would have no difficulty in departing again – whereas if we had come in on a high spring tide then we might have been stuck there for a fortnight.

At last the time came for us to leave Llanes. By then we had grown even more familiar with that dear man, Modesto, and with members of his family. In all honesty I could not pretend I took a great liking to Llanes, probably because it was the scene of such a disaster, but I joined with the others in undying and indeed loving respect for that marvellous little man with the black beret and the sharp humorous features. Every day he made a point of calling on us to make sure we were all right, invariably bringing with him a gift of fish: on one occasion he brought along his young nephew and a friend who spoke English – with the happy result that all our younger crew members had a lively night out at the local disco.

Modesto himself neither drank nor smoked and indeed seemed content to spend most of his time out fishing and we had the greatest difficulty in finding any way of returning his kindness and hospitality. This reticence extended to any claim for his services: when I said I really must pay him something for his invaluable help he kept shrugging and shaking his head, seeming to want nothing. In the end, reluctantly, he accepted a 1,000 peseta note, a pitifully small reward for such invaluable help. However we told him that at least when I got back to England I would write something about him in our yachting press, and so here indeed is my tribute to a true gentleman of the sea, Modesto Garcia of Llanes.

As one last example of this man's inbred courtesy let me finally describe our departure, at four-thirty in the morning. Fortunately it was a beautiful night, and the sea was like a millpond. Because the channel through the outer harbour was still difficult to follow Modesto, who was off himself on an early morning fishing trip, insisted that for the exit he should come aboard *Sanu* and pilot us out – and so it was with his firm hand at the wheel, mine operating the throttle and gears, that *Sanu* at last took her leave.

When we had safely made it to the open sea outside then Modesto's nephew brought their little boat alongside and, with many heartfelt hugs and hand shakes, we said our goodbyes. Even then there was a last touching gesture – for now as we set off along the coast heading ultimately for Santander, for the first two or three miles that tiny Spanish fishing boat kept pace, a few hundred feet starboard of us, winking her lights every now and then, lending us the comforting sense of their human company, until we had once again gained our nautical confidence.

Salute, dear Modesto, good friend and saviour of *Sanu*!

XIII

Arrest on the High Seas

After Llanes almost anywhere would have seemed something
of an anti-climax: not even Santander, for all its bright lights
and lively city centre scattered with museums, was able to
overcome this obstacle. Once again, as with so many of the
Spanish ports we had visited, the entrance was bedevilled with
sandbanks and shallow patches and we had to watch our echo
sounder carefully as we rounded Cabo Mayer and the pretty
little islet of Mouro and then followed the buoyed channel. At
first we hoped to get into the yacht basin in the heart of the city
but this was packed out with boats as we reverted to an earlier
plan to visit the new Marina del Cantabrico, whose
advertisements had been appearing regularly in the English
yachting magazines.

Unfortunately for us the marina proved to be some five
miles outside Santander – though indeed, as we found to the
cost of our ears, a mere three minutes from the airport. At
least we were able to fill up with water and have a shower but
then we became increasingly depressed as we found that
unlike Vilamoura the place had no amenities, not a single food
shop nor even a proper restaurant. Somehow it all seemed
rather ghastly, rows and rows of pontoons occupied by mostly
uninteresting fibreglass yachts, and all around vast empty
spaces which presumably one day would be filled with
apartments. We felt quite lonely and were glad to pay our
night's fee of £7, untie our ropes and motor across to the
bustling fish harbour over at Santander where at least there
was an impression of life going on. We berthed alongside a
fascinating large crabber whose captain told us he was

carrying a load of many tons of live crabs. These were kept in special tanks through which he pumped fresh sea water continually (to keep the crabs alive) so that our night's sleep was hardly a peaceful one. We had a good reason for picking that berth, however, for it was opposite the local Campsana fuel pumps and in the morning we were able to fill up with gas oil. Now we were all ready, or as ready as could be after our many recent problems, for what was to be the longest trip of the whole voyage, 200 miles from Santander across the Bay of Biscay to La Rochelle, in France.

When we finally sailed out past Mouro at about eleven o'clock in the morning I fancy all of us were a little tense, haunted as we were by the knowledge of all those slow leaks plus the suspicion that maybe halfway across our old Kelvin engine just *might* start to misbehave – not to mention our awareness of the notoriously unstable weather record of the Bay. In actual fact we were pretty fortunate: for the first day's sailing the sea was dead calm and, though during the night the wind blew up and we had a strong north-westerly almost sideways on, nevertheless we accomplished our 200 miles with surprising ease – sighting the tall Coubre lighthouse off the entrance to the River Loire at about eleven o'clock the next morning, and from these setting course for La Rochelle.

At Santander Judith had already departed on the ferry to Plymouth, and now Tim and Lyn were due to leave us. They had already booked a rented car from La Rochelle and knowing that the office closed at six o'clock they were naturally anxious to reach the port before then. So were the rest of us: however the local port authorities had decreed that the port only opened to yachts for two hours before and after high tide, so we were left to circle around in the open sea, realising we were unlikely to be able to berth until seven o'clock. Fortunately someone spied a nearby small marina where we were able to land Tim and Lyn, so that they could go off and collect their car. Meantime we continued our circular touring until the magic hour of seven finally arrived and we were able to sail via the buoyed channel into one of France's most lovely harbours, entered under the tall and romantic shadow of the tower of St Nicholas.

Jess and I retained vivid memories of our earlier visit and so we were able to nose our way right into the inner harbour and find a pleasant berth a few yards from the main town street. Unfortunately our memories must have faded on detail for when it came to leaving we found an irascible French lock-keeper demanding from us a sum of £19 for a stay of two days! Since this gentleman had total control of the lock gates and the drawbridge and we were trapped without his aid there was nothing to do but pay up and go with as good a grace as possible.

After La Rochelle we began to feel we were really beginning to get near to home. First however came the pleasure of revisiting two of the many pretty islands which lie conveniently along the coast of Brittany: Ile d'Yeu, where so many years ago Jess and I and the family had hired bicycles and soared up and down those sunny flat lanes, and afterwards Belle Ile, a lovely place which lives up to its name, though now somewhat over-run by tourists. At both islands we put out our wooden leg and leaned against the quay wall and hoped there would be an opportunity to examine our suspect hull, but alas we were caught in neap tides and though *Sanu*'s keel rested firmly on the bottom the water level never fell enough for a real check.

'Never mind,' I said soothingly, 'when we get to Audierne it will be spring tides and I'm sure we'll have time to look at the hull.'

Before reaching Audierne we called in at Concarneau, one of the biggest of the Breton fishing ports with a big fishing fleet nestling under the attractive castle walls. The entrance to Concarneau is not an easy one and we had considerable difficulty in finding the important buoys, especially as since our last visit the French buoyage system appeared to have changed, so that black became green and so on. However, this was child's play in comparison with our subsequent journey from Concarneau to Audierne, involving as it did threading our way between the scattered Iles de Glénan with rocks and islets lying all over the place in gay abandon.

In our case we headed for Ile de Moutones, where we knew there was a three-quarter of a mile wide channel, and after some worrying moments finally found ourselves safely through and able to continue round the rock-strewn coast towards the tall Penmarch Lighthouse which marked the turn for the twenty mile run to Audierne. This latter had always been our favourite Breton port and we had visited it at least half a dozen times in the past. We used to love lying alongside the colourful fishing boats and wandering up and down the cobbled quayside lined with little market stalls. Did we but know all this had been changed by 'progress' and even our favourite old fashioned café had been turned into a posh new hotel ... however before we could make such discoveries we were to be plunged into the second great drama of our voyage.

It happened like this. First, after passing through the Iles de Glénan and setting course for Penmarch we had been rather puzzled to be buzzed by a small spotter aeroplane which circled round several times before flying away. Strange we thought, and then became immersed in the task of rounding Penmarch point ... As we did so we all relaxed over a lunch of bread and cheese and cold beers, sitting on the deck in bright sunshine: the sea had calmed, the sky was blue, oh, it was good to be alive and cruising at last in warm waters.

Although as I have said we had been to Audierne many times, that was ten years back and I was anxious now to make sure I found the entrance correctly as we hugged the coast and, with Uni beside me to double check, I began ticking off landmarks, a water tower here, a church belfry there, and so on, until we pinpointed the familiar breakwater. Like most Breton ports Audierne is best entered around high tide and I had deliberately arranged so that we arrived about an hour before the day's high tide. Even so I knew there was a torturous chancel to follow round to the inner quays and when I saw two or three blue and white Audierne fishing boats heading along the coast, obviously bound for their home port, I decided to play safe and follow them in. As a result all my attention was focussed on bringing *Sanu* round behind the last of the squat familiar boats. And so ...

'Better look out, Denys – the Navy's alongside.'

I thought Uni was joking, but he wasn't. Looking sideways I found *Sanu* heavily over-shadowed by a large grey patrol boat, with eight men in khaki uniforms lining the sides poised to jump aboard. Seeing that they had caught my attention one of the men motioned me to slow down while they came closer.

'What on earth –?' I began.

The next moment there was a bump as the boat came alongside, but nothing to worry about naturally as being the Navy they had dozens of very expensive orange fenders to take the strain. Within seconds they had tied up, and suddenly *Sanu* seemed alive with French sailors. Only they weren't sailors, we discovered, but officers of the Douane, the French Customs.

As it happened my obsession at the time was with getting into port and alongside the Audierne quays so that at low tide we might have a chance to examine our hull. When the officer in charge started addressing me I hardly listened to what he said, but produced a clock, pointing to the time, saying urgently:

'*Monsieur, c'est très important que nous allons à Audierne pour examination de la bâteau pour le – le –*' Unable to think of the French equivalent for the word I repeated several times, to their bewilderment: '*Les* leaks – *comprenez, monsieur*? *Les* leaks.'

Thus, bizarrely, began our historic encounter with the French Navy, or rather to be exact, the naval branch of the Douane. We were completely astonished at what was happening to us, but it soon became apparent that these men were very much in earnest. After we had stood arguing for several minutes in pidgin English and French the captain of the boat came over, and fortunately he spoke English. He was young and good looking but a little too suave for my liking. He explained that he wanted us to follow him to a nearby anchorage where his men would inspect our boat. In vain did I wave my clock and explain our predicament: all he would say was that he quite understood but there was plenty of time.

Well, then there might have been plenty of time. *Two hours later* ... After two hours the men had hardly finished searching our cabin, let alone other parts of the boat. We had no idea what they expected to find but they were certainly thorough in their inspection. Fixing their attentions on the large aft cabin they really turned it upside down, removing half the ballast, upturning beds, opening cupboards, sorting through private belongings. It all seemed like something out of a film and we had to keep pinching ourselves to be sure we weren't dreaming.

Every now and then, stung by anger I would storm up to the captain.

'Look here – *quel est le purpose de votre inspection, monsieur?*'

And again.

'*Nous sommes tourists, monsieur, comprenez? Tourists!*'

It was all to no avail. The captain merely smiled politely while his men went on searching. By now they had moved into the engine room, using long rods to poke down into the fuel tanks, infuriating Bob by emptying the contents of plastic bags in which he had carefully stored a whole lot of spare parts. And all the time the clock ticked on and on …

It made me so angry that I began shouting at the captain, and in the end, seeing I was in earnest, he relented. Very well, he said, we could go into Audierne, but with four of his men aboad, and once there they would require to continue their search while we lay against the quay.

This they certainly did. Attention was now given to other parts, to the saloon, to Genny's bedroom, to our cabin, even to the ancient safety raft on the wheelhouse roof. In point of fact there was nothing aboard the boat out of the ordinary other than our own clothes and a few gifts, plus a couple of cases of Portuguese wine. Technically I suppose we had one or two bottles more than the allowance of 2 bottles per person, but anyway we showed the boxes and they were quickly cast aside, obviously of no interest.

All this took time. Looking at my clock I realised that three and a half hours had elapsed since we were first boarded, and so far there seemed no sign of the search ending. Naturally word had got around the quay at Audierne and a crowd of interested spectators had gathered to watch the drama of the arrested English boat. Some of them probably found it entertaining but by now we were all of us thoroughly exasperated – especially as every time we asked what was the reason for the search the men merely shrugged.

Finally to our astonishment the captain himself donned a diving outfit and informed us he proposed to go below and inspect our hull!

'Ask him to check on our leaks,' said Uni wryly.

The captain was down for quite a while, and we could hear vague and regular tapping noises. What on earth was he up to? I got quite worried, remembering those very temporary patches. What damage might he do?

At last the captain appeared. He looked somehow disappointed, and after some discussion with his comrades announced, rather regretfully we could see, that the search was over. No apology, no explanation, just a brief word to the effect that they would soon be departing – meantime one of his men would give us an official clearance certificate which we could show to any other customs officers who might call.

I was so angry at all this that I thought it best to go downstairs and begin peeling potatoes for our evening meal. Where I stood working happened to be just below where some of the customs men were sitting on the deck, and I could hear them giggling among themselves.

That did it! I flung down the potatoes and scrambled up on to the deck and went straight up to the captain, waving my hands expressively and uttering my hysterical farewell words.

'*Monsieur, vous êtes très amusés – mais* moi, *je ne pas amusé! Vous dites,* Ha! Ha! Ha! *– mais* moi, *je ne pas dis* Ha! Ha! Ha!' I paused almost speechless with rage, and could only manage two more words. '*Vous êtes –*'

There I stuck, unable to think of an epithet bad enough – then with a final gesture of contempt I went off down to the saloon again.

At least apparently my visible show of anger worked, for the others said that the result was most effective. The captain and his men looked quite embarrassed and without another word gathered their belongings and went away, leaving us as mystified about their visit at the end as we had been at the beginning.

Explanation in fact only came a day or two later by which time we had become friendly with the crew of a boat we had tied up alongside. Unlike most of the boats in Audierne this was not a fishing boat but a survey vessel, run by a delightful bunch of young men, French, but English-speaking. They invited us aboard for a drink and it was then we learned what all the fuss had been about. Apparently four days previously a packet of 38 kilos of cannabis had been found floating in the sea somewhere off Concarneau. Not surprisingly the customs had been put on the alert and of course seeing a British MFV cruising over the same route – and later on seeming to behave rather strangely (when I weaved about to tail the Audierne fishing boats) – they became suspicious and decided to stop us and search the boat. They must have imagined they had probably found their quarry, as it gave us great pleasure now to realise how exasperated they must have felt when it dawned on them that they had picked the wrong boat.

All the same the incident left a nasty taste in our mouths and helped to spoil our enjoyment of Audierne – that and the upsetting way the town had been tarted up as a tourist place. We saw none of those old Breton fishermen and their wives in Breton costumes, and the only thing we remembered with real pleasure was a farewell meal in a local pizza bar where we all toasted one another in cool Muscadet wine and saluted a successful conclusion to our voyage, that last formidable leg from Audierne to Falmouth, some 150 miles in all.

Our final disappointment at Audierne was to find the tides wrong for inspecting the hull. However the leaks didn't seem too bad and we decided that in the circumstances the best thing would be to get the boat back home promptly. It was still dark when we left Audierne around six o'clock in the morning but the faint light of impending dawn plus the harbour lamps made it not too difficult to find our way out – as an added precaution we followed a small fishing boat also just leaving. Once in the open sea, we set the old Kelvin at a steady $6\frac{1}{2}$-7 knots an hour and headed *Sanu* for Le Chat lighthouse and the beginning of that straggling line of rocky islets making up the notorious Raz de Sein. In all these extend for more than 20 miles westwards: local fishermen with special knowledge make use of one or two narrow channels to pass through, but in view of our recent unhappy experiences we played safe and headed outwards until we had given a safe clearance to the last major obstacle, the ominously named Amen lighthouse.

Seeing this again, brought back vivid memories of an occasion when we had once been caught in a fog and heard the blast of a fog horn dead ahead of us, slowing up just in time to avoid driving right on to Amen! We found a French fishing boat from Ile de Sein sheltering there and got friendly with them over a bottle of whisky, so much so that they tried to prevail on us to follow them to their home port, but we thought it wisest to carry on for Audierne once the fog had lifted. As we went we took many a thoughtful look back at that huge lighthouse with the name daubed in crimson letters, A-M-E-N, glad that our acquaintance had been brief and not too close.

Once round Amen we changed course to 5 degrees to take us past Ushant and on our way to dear old England. At this stage unfortunately the sea began to get rougher with the waves, as ever, on our side and the journey became very uncomfortable. Nevertheless we were all cheered to see the faint outline of land ahead and knew that this must be Ushant, the very last piece of France we would see on this voyage. Of course it could have been one of the inner islands or even the mainland if we had been badly off course but fortunately as we drew nearer we recognised the several tall lighthouses, La Juvenet and Creach among them, and felt able to relax.

At least we would have relaxed if we had not just then encountered a very violent race, short sharp high waves that seemed to leap up to meet us. Poor old *Sanu* began rearing about like a bucking bronco and it was all I could do to hold the wheel steady. I don't think for a long time have I experienced such an uncomfortable half hour or so until at long last Creach tower began to fall behind us and the sea settled down into its former semi-rough state.

At this moment it would have been nice to have added 'and then we had an uneventful 100 mile trip back to Falmouth', but the Fates had not finished with us. As it was time for the BBC mid-day shipping forecast we switched on the radio. The morning forecast had been a good one, something like Force 4 veering to Force 5 south-westerly, which meant we might have the waves partly behind us. However now we heard the announcer say abruptly: 'Here is a gale warning for the Plymouth Area – Force 7 increasing to Force 8 gale.' Plymouth, needless to say, was the area we were heading for!

Ah well, there was little we could do now, too late to turn back, the only thing was to keep going and hope perhaps we could race the gale to Falmouth.

'How are the bilges, Bob?' I said casually.

'OK,' said Bob. 'The pumps are coping very well.'

He didn't add 'under the circumstances' but he could well have done. Not surprisingly under the impending conditions of a gale there were quite a few reasons for us to feel more than a little worried. First and foremost, the waves and the wind appeared to be coming mainly from the west, that is on our port side, and that was where most of our leaks had developed: even now an occasional big wave crashed against the hull and such poundings were not going to do our leaks any good at all. More than once I took a hasty peep downstairs under the floorboards but thankfully all seemed well.

Second, there was the ever present problem of our Kelvin engine, two of whose bearings had gone at Leixeos: although these had been fixed and since then Bob had done a marvellous job of nursing the engine along, it remained a potential worry.

Third and finally there was the closely related problem of fuel: the expenses of the trip had been wildly increased by all our unexpected hold-ups with the result that we arrived at Audierne with funds at rock bottom. Taking stock of our fuel position we found we had about one hundred gallons in the main tank plus a further twenty in the small auxiliary tank designed for running the Lister side engine in an emergency,

should the main tanks fall too low. Theoretically we would
expect to use about 70 gallons on the trip, so all should be
well; all the same it did seem to be running things a bit close
and at the last moment I had rushed off in a taxi at Audierne
to bring aboard an extra ten gallons as a precaution. Even so
now as we rocked about in the rough seas we could not help
realising that such a shaking would stir up all the dirt at the
bottom of the fuel tanks, with the ever present possibility of a
blocked fuel line.

As darkness fell that evening so did the spirits of the weary
crew of *Sanu* – to be lightened momentarily by the appearance
of a meal of almost classical proportions which somehow
Genevieve had doggedly produced from down in the saloon.
How she did it I shall never quite know but the hot food was
greatly appreciated, even though quite a few portions were
hurled about the wheelhouse by some extra big wave. During
most night trips, or indeed any long day trip, we usually seem
to gather in *Sanu*'s wheelhouse, which is cosy if rather
confined. I suppose in some way we are seeking the comfort of
each other's presence. Either way companionship was a real
comfort now as the wind began to howl, the waves to rise up in
huge white crests, the boat toss around madly, and we all
realised starkly that our very lives were now in the lap of
whatever gods there might be out there in the wild dark night.

Until, that is, we managed to see the first wonderful wink of
the famous Lizard Lighthouse, that beacon of hope which has
greeted so many home-coming sailors. One – two – three, One
– two – three – yes, there it was, for sure.

'The Lizard!' I cried out excitedly. 'I can see the Lizard!'

Then I must confess I dared to hope our troubles were over,
even though I knew we must still be about twenty miles or so
from the land.

I had reckoned without those wayward gods, though.
Suddenly the Kelvin, which had been pounding along
magnificently, missed a beat, and then another, and after a
while stopped altogether. Quickly Bob put on the Lister and
we resumed progress, but this time with agonising slowness as
the Lister only gives us three knots and in such seas perhaps

even less. After a while Bob got the Kelvin going again (the trouble being the inevitable one, fuel blockages), but then it stopped again. After two more such experiences Bob put a new fuel filter on and this seemed to cure the trouble – 'for the time being, anyway' to use Bob's cautious words.

In this manner, caught up now by the increasing force of what must be the gale itself we continued to head towards that familiar winking light. One – two – three – nearer and nearer it came, reassuring at first, until a new worry arose. Because of the engine stoppage we had lost our ability to rely on covering seven miles an hour, consequently we could no longer be sure how close we were to the Lizard lighthouse. We had a Seafix direction finder aboard on which now we could get the Lizard signal very loudly indeed, and of course at a pinch one could home in on that – but when to change direction? Peering through the night both Genevieve and I had the uneasy suspicion that we were already closer than was healthy, remembering as we both did from the past all those jagged rocks around the point.

'Can't we turn for St Anthony Head now?'

Unfortunately there was still no sign of the St Anthony Head light marking the entrance to Falmouth harbour and without that guidance it seemed a little hazardous to turn in on spec as it were. I couldn't, in my tired state, think of any better or at least safer solution than to circle around where we were until daylight came and (as I fondly imagined) we could recognise where we were. We did just this for a time, naturally using the bright winking light of the Lizard as the king-pin of our manoeuvring, and all went well for a time. Then –

'The Lizard!' I cried out incredulously. 'Where's the Lizard light? It's gone – I just can't see it *anywhere.*'

Incredible as it might seem the most powerful lighthouse beam in the entire British Isles had been obliterated in a second – it was literally nowhere to be seen, no matter how hard we searched. What had happened, though we did not appreciate it at the time, was that a thick blanket of fog had descended on the peninsula on which the big white lighthouse was situated. The fog, however, had not extended to the sea, with the result (fortunately) that we could see all the bright navigational lights of the dozens of big ships heading up and down one of the busiest sea lanes in the world. As at the moment we were carrying out steady wide circles right across part of these lanes it behoved us pretty smartly to edge out of the way before we were well and truly rammed by one of those huge oil tankers which, reputedly, take two miles to stop! This we promptly did, there to wait patiently for the uneasy dawn ...

Uneasy it proved to be, too, for with it came not relief but a real extension of the fog plus a blustery wind and even occasional showers of rain. Surely the gods could not do us any more harm?

We debated what best to do. We could no more see the Lizard by day than we had been able to do at night. Well at least we knew in which direction Falmouth lay, due north.

'Let's set a course of 360,' I said. 'We're bound to hit land ...'

Although this was a logical decision we remained uneasy as we peered through mist and rain trying to identify somewhere – then, thank goodness, at long last we saw the bright winking light of the Manacles Light Buoy, and now we knew where we were. The appearance of two large cargo boats obviously just out of Falmouth docks increased our confidence. Finally at about seven thirty we managed to catch the last flickering of St Anthony Head light before it shut off and found ourselves heading for Black Rock and the entrance to the Carrick Roads. What a relief!

After that we knew we were home and safe, if not exactly dry. Mylor Yacht Harbour was in fact only some two miles ahead and as despite all our difficulties we had managed to come in only an hour after high tide we knew there was plenty of water to enable us to cross the shallow-banked entrance, indeed there would be nearly twenty feet in most places.

And so, after a journey of nearly 1,500 miles from the sunny shores of the Algarve, after a night pounding through a Gale Force 8 gale and a morning peering through fog and rain, at last the good ship *Sanu* cruised in among the rows of moored yachts at Mylor, came round in a big sweep and edged up to the new quay where we had booked our berth. Home again from the sea was the wanderer – home after ten long years!

XIV

Home and Dry Again

Usually at the end of each summer's cruise on *Sanu* we have tucked her away at some foreign boatyard or marina and flown home to a period of blissful forgetfulness. After eight weeks' solid life aboard – and it is a life which brooks no rival preoccupations, every day a new challenge, not the least if it happens to be your cookday! – there is a sudden burning desire to exchange the vagaries of life on the ocean wave for the different experiences of life back on land.

Ironically, this year when at last we had managed to get our old boat back to England itself, for the first time we were unable to enjoy this sense of complete relaxation. The reason, of course, to paraphrase one of T.S. Eliot's most famous lines, is that our voyage ended 'not with a bang but with a leak'. Once we had settled into our new berth at Mylor it became only too evident, indeed ominously so, that there was no way in which we could just pack our bags and return to the Mill House and forget all about *Sanu* for a few months. Judging by the rate which water was not merely seeping it but in one or two cases almost pouring in it was going to require a good deal of hasty patching up before we could even think of leaving the boat at all. And indeed, though we immediately rang up Demelza and her friend Diane at the Mill, and they drove over to see us, we saw quite clearly that we would have to stay aboard a day or two before even thinking of going home. Fortunately there was a chance for a leisurely chat over lunch as there was nothing we could do to the boat's hull until the tide had gone out, which it would do for a couple of hours around low tide.

Once the tide had departed we put a ladder over the side,
Uni donned his famous old navy blue overalls and work
began. We had already been able to pinpoint most of the
major leaks and now, armed with mastic and a caulking gun
and some red lead and putty Uni, with Bob's assistance, was
soon filling up various cracks and splits, here and there
covering the repair with the added protection of thin wooden
battens. It was the same kind of repair that had been done at
Llanes – indeed poor *Sanu*'s bottom was beginning to resemble
that of some oft-wounded animal, there were so many strips of
wood and large patches. We were all of us worried at the
implications, but for the moment there seemed nothing we
could do more than seek to stop the inflow of water – later on
we would have to think more seriously about a long term
solution.

While the men were working on the outside, Jess and
Genevieve began the equally arduous task of tidying up the
innards. Although we had this year managed to reduce the
deck leaks (which have plagued us for years) rain was still
tending to scatter over the saloon and seep into one or two
cabins. I was convinced that the only permanent solution
would be a return to Dekaplex, a plastic paint we used to
apply every year, but it was terribly expensive, and like many
other things, for the moment would have to wait. Meantime,
Jess and Genny totally cleared out the food cupboards,
stacked up the mattresses, and finally spread our new canopy
over the whole of the suspect wheelhouse roof, thus ensuring
that at least one part of the boat would remain dry.

Altogether we stayed nearly three days at Mylor before
finally returning home, and this gave us time to look around
Sanu's new berth. It seemed a very beautiful setting, long rows
of yachts swinging to their moorings, wooded hills in all
directions, the main River Fal swirling by on its journey to
Truro – yes we could not have asked for a more tranquil
background, including the moss-covered ancient church of
Mylor just across from the boatyard entrance. The harbour
had a chandlery and other yachting services, and there was a
pleasant restaurant, though unfortunately no food shop and,

saddest of all, no snug old village pub, something we would have welcomed.

There was a yacht club bar but somehow this was not quite the thing, being mainly occupied by elderly gentlemen carefully decked up in oilskins and yellow wellingtons rather like characters in some play. Having travelled nearly 30,000 miles in our old boat and come across yachting types the world over we remained profoundly unimpressed by them – in our experience the best, and certainly the most interesting nautical travellers are much more likely to be clad in jeans and old jerseys, and quite possibly liberally sprinkled with diesel oil! However, be that as it may, Mylor Yacht Harbour looked a snug enough home base for a rather weary traveller from the antique lands of the Mediterranean.

When we finally drove from Mylor home to the Mill House we had by no means totally conquered the leaks and water was still coming in fairly steadily, but we thought we would be safe in leaving the boat for three days, before returning for a check-up. In this assumption we were a few vital hours out – by the time we returned the water was up around the engine and we had to quickly put the pumps on and then clean out the oil sump and gear box. This prompted me to try out an idea we had discussed and I raced back into Penryn to buy an automatic switch for our electric pump which Bob at once installed. We tested this out before leaving, and felt reasonably confident that this time the inflow of water would be stemmed, and this time, fortunately we were right.

Next time we returned to the boat we could actually hear the pump switching on for one of its periodical emptyings, and there was very little water in the bilges. All the same there were still a few uncured leaks and on the next really high spring tide we came over in full force and spent four hours down on the ground ferreting among *Sanu*'s large hull, applying yet more patches. After that we felt, hopefully, we could settle down to a system of weekly visits, until perhaps early in the spring, we could arrange to take *Sanu* into a boatyard and have a major overhaul. We didn't think it was too serious, but obviously she required refastening in places, and a complete recaulking. After all, nothing like that had been done for more than ten years, and all these seasons in the glaring Mediterranean sunshine hadn't done the planking any good.

At last, at long last, we were able to turn our minds from Mylor to the Mill House. Here, too, dramas had been taking place. Alas, my fond dreams of family harmony through a gathering of the clan for the summer holidays had gone woefully wrong. Perhaps because they were deprived of our moderating influence, various members had fallen out and indeed, it seemed, practically come to blows. We had excited, though rather saddening pictures of one person standing brandishing a pitchfork and another a log of wood: what were we coming to? This was meant to be a peaceful unit in a world of violence! It all seemed very petty and a pity that a few precious weeks of summer holidays should be wasted in such squabbles, but Jess and I felt there was little we could do about it.

Paradoxically, in the midst of hearing of all this aggro, we found the Mill House at its most beautiful. After all our disappointing weeks of bad weather, suddenly we were enjoying a beautiful Cornish autumn. The sun shone, everything was at its greenest, prior to the impending autumnal fading – the giant rhubarb plants were bigger than ever, the trees swarmed with rooks, vegetation was lush in all directions. Diane had mown the lawn in our honour and so we were able to sit in splendour eating lunch in the sunshine. At least – we and a few others, for the fact was that, in that not over subtle way which seems almost a regular feature of 'life at the mill', Demelza and Diane had acquired a few followers.

Temporarily staying in Stephen's chalet we found Julia, a member of the Barneys, a travelling road show which we had once seen perform at Rosie's wine bar, and which had been appearing at the recent Festival of Fools at Penzance. Also around was Sue, an Australian friend and now, of course, in addition to Jess, Genny and me, there were Bob and Uni, our faithful crewmen, from whom it seemed hard to part; they had been such good friends and so helpful that we felt the least we could do was offer them a bit of hospitality on *terra firma*. Next to arrive to say 'hullo' was Martin, at the moment immersed in his annual St Ives Festival, looking indeed far more worn and washed out by his administrative problems than any of us. He said we simply must make the effort to attend the last night of the Festival, where Bob Kerr and his Whoopee Band were playing at the Guildhall, and that we did manage, the whole crowd of us.

It was good for a moment to be back in St Ives, with a bright moon shining on the harbour waters and illuminating the familiar ever romantic outline of the Island, and the long line of waves creeping up 'our' old beach of Porthmeor. How many light years ago was it since we lived at St Christophers and brought up six small children ...? Now several of them were into their thirties, had husbands and children: indeed only the previous day Gill had given birth to her third daughter, making the quota of grandchildren eight. Life goes on ...

When we returned from the Festival and suddenly found our numbers increased by the temporary presence, partly in our house and partly in Stephen's chalet, of a complete rock band – well Jess and I did begin to feel a bit fed up. During the long trip I suppose we had rather been looking forward to a spell of peace and quiet, maybe with rosy visions of a white-haired old couple sitting around a log fire, etc. etc. Instead we found ourselves part of a collection that for one single night (when unexpectedly four friends of Bob's turned up at midnight) reached the grand total of seventeen human beings!

'Do you think we could go away for a holiday?' said Jess wistfully.

It was indeed too much: but fortunately within two or three days the band had gone, plus several others, and suddenly we were back to normal. Bob was returning to London, and we were sad to see him go: he had been a stalwart companion through all our nautical adventures, and almost alone had nursed the old Kelvin safely back to England. We could never adequately repay him for that generous service he gave as a natural part of his character – we just hoped very much he would find some new and equally absorbing interest.

Uni, on the other hand, or so it then seemed, looked like having been once again overcome by Cornwall's insidious appeal and all being well was going to stay over the winter and help to do a lot of jobs, like cutting wood and getting the wheel going, which in the past had been Stephen's prerogative. He, by the way, was still over in Ireland helping his friend Michael Penhaligan to build up an old Irish cottage which had been left to Michael. Stephen's wife Gina and their children had gone back to America and we supposed Stephen would be following in due course, but for the moment, to judge by a few ecstatic postcards from Ireland, he was enjoying his taste of the land of the blarney. And why not indeed? – 'tis a lovely land.

And so, quite pleasantly, life began to slip back into its more normal pattern. Once again I was able to see my old friend Bill Picard for a lunchtime drink in the St John's House, once more, ever hopeful, Jess set out to conduct her weekly WEA classes on psychology, once more there were walks on the windblown sands of Sennen beach or up on the lonely moors around Trencrom or Ding Dong – and once more, one of my favourite occasions, most Sunday nights we would have a big family gathering for the evening meal, perhaps nine or ten of us at our round table, Demelza and Diane and Genevieve, Jess and I, Martin over for the day, perhaps Jane and Rick or Alan and Gill down for a weekend.

Yes, I was glad to think, things are getting back to normal. Slowly visions of alarums at Llanes harbour and invasions by French customs officers, not forgetting 24 hours of gale force winds crossing the Channel – slowly such disturbing visions faded into the background, and once more we were able to feel at home again among the greenery of the Mill House, and to the ever present background of the gurgling stream wandering lazily down to the sea ...